BACH...
Single Docto...

At work they are skilled medical
professionals, but at home, as soon as they
walk in the door, these eligible bachelors are
on full-time fatherhood duty!

**These devoted dads still find room in their
lives for love…**

It takes very special women to win the hearts
of these dedicated doctors, and a very special
kind of caring to make these single fathers
full-time husbands!

**Look out for the next book in this
mini-series—coming soon from
Jennifer Taylor and Medical Romance™!**

Jennifer Taylor lives in the north-west of England with her husband Bill. She had been writing Mills & Boon® romances for some years, but when she discovered Medical Romances™ she was so captivated by these heart-warming stories that she set out to write them herself! When she's not writing, or doing research for her latest book, Jennifer's hobbies include reading, travel, walking her dog and retail therapy (shopping!). Jennifer claims all that bending and stretching to reach the shelves is the best exercise possible. She's always delighted to hear from readers, so do visit her at www.jennifer-taylor.com

THE CONSULTANT'S ADOPTED SON

BY
JENNIFER TAYLOR

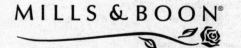

MILLS & BOON®

All the characters in this book have no existence outside the imagination of the author, and have no relation whatsoever to anyone bearing the same name or names. They are not even distantly inspired by any individual known or unknown to the author, and all the incidents are pure invention.

First published in Great Britain 2006
Harlequin Mills & Boon Limited,
Eton House, 18-24 Paradise Road, Richmond, Surrey TW9 1SR

© Jennifer Taylor 2006

ISBN 0 263 84730 6

Set in Times Roman 10¼ on 12 pt.
03-0506-58598

Printed and bound in Spain
by Litografia Rosés, S.A., Barcelona

CHAPTER ONE

HE KNEW who she was as soon as she came through the door. Even though they'd never met before, he recognised her. Her hair was the exact same honey-gold colour as Daniel's was, and the way she tilted her head to the side as she looked around the bar was exactly what his son would have done, too.

Owen Gallagher's hand clenched around his glass. He'd tried to prepare himself for this meeting, but seeing the resemblance between this woman and Daniel made him realise how dangerous the situation really was. If he wasn't careful he could end up losing his son, and the thought was more than he could bear. He loved Daniel more than anything in the world and he wouldn't allow anyone to take him away from him!

A crowd of people suddenly came into the pub and the woman disappeared from view. Owen cursed as he stood up and tried to see where she had gone. He should have made himself known to her as soon as she'd arrived instead of sitting here, worrying about what might or might not happen.

Normally, he wasn't someone who hesitated. He couldn't afford to be in his job, when he needed to make life-and-death decisions. He was used to trusting his instincts, yet he was afraid to trust them now. He was too closely involved in this situation and it would be foolish to hope that instinct alone would guide him down the right path. He needed to follow his head, not his heart, although it wasn't going to be easy to detach himself emotionally when Daniel's whole future depended on him making the right decisions.

The crowd suddenly parted and he breathed a sigh of relief when he saw the woman walking to the bar. He made his way towards her, using the few seconds it took to take stock. She was taller than he'd imagined, and slimmer, too. She was wearing a black trouser suit with a white blouse and a pair of low-heeled black shoes. Although her clothes were very neat and tidy, he could tell they weren't expensive from the cut of the jacket—it was a little too loose around her waist and the sleeves were an inch too long. She stopped at the bar and he paused, too, needing another few seconds before he introduced himself.

Her face was in profile now, and his heart lurched as he studied the smooth curve of her brow, the straight line of her nose and the fullness of her lips. She was even more like Daniel in profile, and it was unsettling to see the familiar features on her face. It wasn't easy to control the feeling of panic that was creeping up on him, but he'd never been a coward and he refused to behave like one now. This woman had the power to disrupt Daniel's life. If he had to conquer his own fears to ensure that wouldn't happen, that was what he would do.

Owen's gaze moved on as he made himself take stock of the glossy fall of honey-gold hair that swung around her shoulders. Her hair was very thick and straight, like a golden waterfall as it shimmered in the lights above the bar. When she bent over to take her purse out of her bag, he half reached towards her, curious to see if her hair felt as cool and as smooth as it looked, before he realised what he was doing.

His hand fell to his side and he breathed in sharply to clear his head. It didn't matter how her hair felt. It only mattered how it looked, and it looked exactly the same as Daniel's did, apart from its length. The sooner he accepted these similarities, the easier it would be to discount them. He couldn't afford to focus on the resemblance between them otherwise he wouldn't be able to separate himself emotionally from what needed to be done. He might not know anything about her, but he did know one thing: she was a threat.

She suddenly turned, and Owen felt a rush of panic assail him when her eyes locked with his. He wasn't mentally prepared yet to speak to her and wasn't sure what he should do. Should he introduce himself now, or should he wait a while longer?

'Excuse me.'

Her voice was low, husky, and the hair on the back of his neck lifted when he heard it for the very first time. So far, they'd only communicated by letter—a terse little note from him suggesting they should meet, an even shorter reply from her, agreeing to the idea. He hadn't thought about how she would sound, so it came as a shock to realise that he found the husky tones very appealing.

He stepped aside to let her pass, feeling goose-bumps break out all over his skin when she murmured her thanks. All of a sudden it felt as though there wasn't enough air in the pub and he couldn't breathe. He hurried to the door. His only thought was to escape from a situation that was turning out to be far more stressful than he'd anticipated it would be. But even as he reached for the handle he knew he couldn't leave. Not yet. Not until he'd made her understand what was going to happen.

He took a deep breath, filled his lungs with the heavy, turgid air, then turned around. If ever there was a time when he needed to be in control of himself, it was now.

Rose found an empty table and sat down. Taking a cardboard coaster out of the ashtray, she carefully placed her glass on it. She really hadn't wanted a drink. She'd bought it simply because it had been expected of her. When you went into a pub you bought a drink. That was it, all nice and tidy—unlike her life, which was turning into such a mess.

A spasm of dread shot through her and she picked up the glass and sipped a little of the wine, hoping it would steady her. Ever since she had agreed to this meeting she'd worried about what was going to happen. She'd gone over it in her head, time and time again, but it had been pure guesswork, of course.

She had no real idea what Owen Gallagher wanted to see her about, except that it had something to do with Daniel—the child she'd given up for adoption eighteen years ago. Not a day had gone by since then when she hadn't thought about him, worried about him, wondered where he was and if he was happy. Was that what Owen Gallagher wanted to know—if she ever thought about the child she'd given away?

She hoped so, because it would be the easiest thing in the world to tell him the truth. She'd never stopped thinking about Daniel, had never stopped regretting the circumstances that had forced her to give him up. Even though she was sure that she'd made the right decision, she had many regrets, but was that really what Owen Gallagher wanted to hear? Or was there another reason why he'd contacted her?

Rose put the glass back on the coaster as her hand began to tremble. She'd refused to allow herself to go beyond this point before, refused to consider the idea that Daniel might be ill and that was why Gallagher had tracked her down. One read about such things all the time—mothers and the children they'd given away reunited through illness—but she couldn't accept that was the reason for this meeting. She simply couldn't bear to imagine that her precious child might be desperately ill…

She shot to her feet, unable to sit there while thoughts like that tormented her. Gallagher had asked her to meet him at seven o'clock and it was ten minutes past the hour now. Maybe he'd decided not to come? In that case, there was no point her sitting here in this noisy pub…

'Ms Tremayne? I'm Owen Gallagher. Thank you for agreeing to meet me.'

All of a sudden he was standing in front of her and Rose gasped. 'But I just bumped into you at the bar!'

'Yes. Please, sit down.'

He gestured towards the chair she'd vacated. Rose sat, simply because she couldn't think what else to do. Why hadn't he introduced himself before? she wondered. Why had he stood there, staring at her that way?

Oh, she'd noticed him, of course. Who wouldn't? Even in this crowd he stood out. Tall and dark, with the kind of cleanly hewn good looks that would have appealed to any woman, Owen Gallagher wasn't a man one could ignore. She shot him a careful look as he sat down, taking note of the beautifully tailored grey suit, the crisp white shirt, the silk tie and aura of affluence that surrounded him, and shivered. He wasn't a man to be ignored—or crossed, for that matter—and it wasn't pleasant to wonder what he wanted with her.

'I may as well get straight to the point, Ms Tremayne. Eighteen years ago my late wife and I adopted your son.'

'Your *late* wife?' Rose put in hurriedly. 'You mean she's dead?'

'Yes. Laura died two years ago, after a long illness.' He didn't appear unduly upset about having to relay the news, but Rose had dealt with too many people who'd suffered a loss to take that at face value.

'I'm sorry,' she said quietly. 'It must have been a difficult time—for you and for Daniel.'

'It was.' Something flashed in his pewter-coloured eyes, a hint of surprise, possibly, because she'd realised that he was still grieving. Nevertheless, his tone was just as brisk when he continued.

'Daniel was very close to his mother and Laura's death was a massive blow to him. I think that's what set him on his present course, in fact.' He shrugged, his broad shoulders moving lightly under the expensive fabric. 'If Laura had still been alive then I'm sure that things would have been very different today.

Daniel certainly wouldn't have got this ridiculous idea into his head about getting in touch with you.'

'Getting in touch with me?' Rose felt the room tilt and grasped hold of the table. Owen Gallagher had asked her to meet him not because their son was ill but because Daniel wanted to see her?

Her heart ricocheted around her chest as the thought sank in, although it wasn't just the fact that Daniel had decided to contact her that shocked her. It was the way she had linked herself and Owen Gallagher together with that phrase: their son. It made her feel very odd, but she didn't dwell on it because he was speaking again.

'That's right, and before we go any further, Ms Tremayne, I may as well tell you that I am totally opposed to the idea. You have played no part in Daniel's life to this point and I cannot see any reason why you should play a part in it in the future. That's why I wanted to see you tonight—so there would be no mistake about this.'

'What do you mean by that?' Rose sat up straighter. Maybe she was overreacting, but there'd been something in his voice that had turned that statement into a threat.

'I don't want you interfering in Daniel's life. He's been through a rough couple of years and he's still very vulnerable. At the present time he's studying for his A-level exams and I don't intend to allow you to disrupt his life when it's essential that he remains focused.'

'*You* won't allow it?' she said incredulously. 'I'm sorry, but you seem to think that you have some kind of divine right over what Daniel does. If he wants to contact me, that's his choice. It has nothing to do with you.'

'Which proves how little you know about being a parent.'

His deep voice was harsh, the words biting into her and causing maximum pain, but Rose knew that he didn't care if he was hurting her. He only cared about his son, or rather what *he* thought was right for Daniel. He didn't accept that Daniel had to make his own decision regarding this issue. He wanted to dictate what would happen. However, there was no way that she was letting him dictate to her!

'I might not know very much about what it takes to be a good parent, Mr Gallagher, but I do know that if you prevent Daniel from contacting me, it could backfire on you. He will resent you interfering and that could cause a rift between you.'

'I think I know Daniel rather better than you do, Ms Tremayne. He's been through a very harrowing time, and what he needs more than anything else is stability in his life. Meeting you—his birth mother—for the first time would be far too stressful for him.'

'But can't you see that it might help him if he got to know me? He'd be able to get some sense of who he is and where he came from. That could only be a good thing.'

'Or it could unsettle him even more. The fact is that Daniel is in no fit state to make major decisions like this at the moment. It's taken months of hard work to get him to this stage, and I don't intend to stand aside and watch you ruin everything.'

'That's a ridiculous thing to say! Why would I want to ruin anything? I want what is best for Daniel, too. How do you think he's going to feel if I refuse to meet him? Surely that will cause him far more distress?'

'He might be upset at first, but he'll get over it. After all, he doesn't know anything about you apart from the fact that you gave him up for adoption. You are a stranger to him, and that's how I intend the situation to continue.'

'But it isn't up to you, is it? It's Daniel's decision.' She stared him straight in the eyes. There was no way that he was going to browbeat her into submission when her son's happiness was at stake. 'I'm sorry, Mr Gallagher, but I have no intention of turning my back on Daniel. If he contacts me then I shall arrange to see him.'

'Even though I've explained the damage it could cause?'

'Yes, because I don't agree with your assessment. I think that meeting me might help Daniel come to terms with what has happened.'

'I don't think that meeting you will make up for losing his mother. Daniel adored Laura, so if you're harbouring any hopes that he will see you as a substitute you can forget them. It's far more likely that he will be bitterly disappointed when you don't live up to his expectations.'

'That's a risk I shall have to take,' she said quietly, not wanting him to know how much the comment had hurt.

'But it's a risk I am not prepared to take, Ms Tremayne.'

He leant across the table, looking big and intimidating as he stared at her. Rose felt a flurry of fear unfurl in the pit of her stomach. She knew she would regret making an enemy of him but she refused to back down. She'd not been able to do anything for her son apart from making sure that he was well cared for, but she could do this for him now. She could find the courage to fight this man and give Daniel the freedom to choose what he wanted.

'Are you threatening me, Mr Gallagher? Because I have to say that it sounded very much like it to me. However, if it *was* a threat then you should know that I don't respond to being threatened.'

'It wasn't a threat, Ms Tremayne. It was merely a statement of intent. I am not prepared to let you ruin my son's life.'

'I see.' She gave a bitter little laugh. 'You seem to have made up your mind about me, don't you? You've decided that I'm not a fit person to be in contact with Daniel, yet you have no basis whatsoever for thinking that I will cause him any harm.'

'Neither do I have any reason to believe that you will help him,' he said flatly. 'You gave him away, Ms Tremayne, so surely that proves how little he means to you? Why bother getting involved at this point when it will only cause a lot of heartache for everyone concerned? And if you are willing to co-operate with me over this, I am prepared to be very generous.'

'*Generous...* What do you mean?'

Rose's head was spinning again. She could scarcely believe what she was hearing. Didn't he realise how hard it had been to give away her precious child, the baby she'd nurtured inside her for all those months? Even now, eighteen years later, she still woke up in tears sometimes, remembering how it had felt in the weeks following her decision to have Daniel adopted. Only women who had been through such an experience could understand the sense of loss that had filled her. Her body had *ached* for her child, and her mind, too. She had grieved for her baby even though he hadn't died, and yet this man had the temerity to accuse her of not caring.

'What do you mean?' she repeated, her voice rising so that the couple at the next table turned and stared at them.

'Please, keep your voice down.' Owen Gallagher's expression darkened as he leant closer to her. 'You might enjoy making a scene, but I don't. I came here tonight to tell you that I don't want you making contact with my son, not to have an argument. Daniel has already written to you. I managed to persuade him to delay posting his letter for a week while he thinks about what he's doing, but that was as far as I got. However, maybe I can convince you to take a more reasonable view.'

He felt in his inside pocket and pulled out a thick brown envelope. 'There is five thousand pounds in here, and it's yours if you give me your word that you won't make any attempt to reply to his letter.'

He placed the envelope in the centre of the table. Rose stared at it in horror. He really thought that he could bribe her into complying with his demands?

'I don't want your money!' She shoved the envelope back at him and stood up, feeling the hot sting of tears in her eyes.

She blinked them away because she wouldn't give him the satisfaction of seeing her cry.

'It might surprise you to learn that I can't be bought off, so please don't make the mistake of trying this again, Mr Gallagher. I would hate Daniel to know the lengths to which you will go to get what you want.'

She brushed past him, forcing her way through the crowd that had gathered around the bar. One man tried to grab hold of her as she passed but Rose shrugged him off, ignoring the catcalls that followed her out of the door. She didn't care what people called her. Foul names couldn't hurt her; they certainly couldn't cause the kind of heartache she was currently feeling.

There was a bus coming along the road so she ran to the stop and flagged it down. She paid her fare and sat down. The bus stopped again to let a car out of the pub's car park and her heart began to thump when she recognised the driver of the expensive vehicle as Owen Gallagher.

He glanced around to check the road was clear and Rose's heart beat even harder when she saw the expression on his face. She had never seen anyone who looked as tortured as he did at that moment. He looked like a man *in extremis,* and the thought that she was responsible for all that pain was very difficult to bear.

She sat back in the seat as he drove away. She knew that she'd made herself an enemy that day and it was the last thing she'd wanted to do. She had no idea what would happen now, but one thing was certain: Owen Gallagher would do everything in his power to keep Daniel away from her.

'Sorry about this. I was all set to give you the grand tour when all hell broke loose. There should be an empty locker in here, so once you've put your coat away can you come straight through? I'll have to fill you in as and when I get the chance.'

Rose sighed as the charge nurse hurried away. Although she

was used to the frenetic pace of a busy accident and emergency department, it would have been nice if there'd been time for someone to show her around for a change.

Opening the staffroom door, she went in and looked around. It was a typical hospital staffroom, from the pile of mugs stacked up on the draining board to the row of metal lockers lined up against the wall. She'd seen hundreds of similar staffrooms since she'd been working for the nursing agency, so she wasn't sure why the sight depressed her so much that day. Maybe it was because she'd felt so downhearted ever since the night she'd met Owen Gallagher in the pub?

Rose grimaced as she took off her coat and hung it up in one of the empty lockers. Over a week had passed since that night, yet the memory still weighed heavily on her. Granted, she'd been angry at the way Gallagher had tried to bribe her, but it had been that glimpse of his face as he'd driven away that had bothered her most, surprisingly enough. She didn't enjoy hurting people even though he had treated her so shabbily. She'd thought about writing to him yet what could she have said? That she hadn't wanted to upset him? *Oh, please!*

Rose's pretty mouth compressed as she made her way to the treatment area. The charge nurse was on the telephone and she held up her hand when Rose approached her. It was another couple of seconds before she hung up, and Rose could tell immediately that something major was about to happen.

'RTA on its way,' the charge nurse explained, bustling past her. 'Multiple casualties, with an ETA of four minutes, so we need to get everything set up. You've worked in Resus before, I hope?'

'Many times,' Rose replied, following the other woman across the foyer. It was just gone seven a.m. and already the waiting room was filling up. Swingeing cuts to health-care budgets had resulted in many of the smaller emergency departments closing their doors. Casualties were brought to central points and St Anne's was one of the biggest in this part of London. That it was reputed to be one of the best was the reason why she had been so keen to work there.

'I've worked in just about every A and E in central London. I've also done the extra training required for trauma care,' she explained as the charge nurse led the way into the resuscitation room, which was where the most critically injured patients were treated.

'Really?' The other woman looked relieved. 'Looks like we've struck gold for once. I can't count the number of times we've ended up with agency staff who don't know the first thing about A and E work. At least we'll be spared our revered boss having an apoplectic fit today…'

She broke off when a nurse popped her head round the door to warn them the first ambulance had arrived. Turning back to Rose, she said hurriedly, 'Find out where everything is, can you? Once the patients start arriving, there won't be time to direct you.'

Rose took a deep breath as the other nurse hurried away. It wasn't the first time she'd been dropped in at the deep end, neither would it be the last. Every time she worked at a new hospital she had to acquaint herself with the layout of the department. Just for a second she thought wistfully how wonderful it would be if she had a permanent post to go to each day, before she dismissed the idea. Agency work paid double the salary she could earn in a permanent job, and that had to be the major consideration at the moment.

She did a quick tour of the room, taking note of where all the supplies were kept. It was obviously a new facility because the equipment was the most modern she'd seen. She cast an admiring glance at the state-of-the-art radiography equipment, which was linked to a sophisticated computer system—there'd be no waiting around for X-ray films to be developed here!

'Male, aged seventeen, with extensive leg injuries.'

The doors crashed open as the paramedics wheeled in the first patient and Rose ran to help. She listened attentively as they rattled out details about the young man's BP and oxygen saturation levels, the amount of saline fluid he'd received as well as the drugs that had been administered. Even the smallest detail could turn out to be important, so she made sure that she didn't miss anything as she positioned herself at the top right corner of the specially adapted trauma bed.

'On my count…one, two…!'

Rose grabbed a corner of the spinal board when one of the crew started to count and helped to lift the young man off the trolley. The charge nurse was standing at the foot of the bed and she glanced at her.

'Get rid of his clothes, will you? The consultant's on his way… Ah, speak of the devil. Here he is.'

Rose looked round as the doors burst open again. She heard the other nurse say something to her but the words seemed to be coming from a distance. All she could see was the man striding towards her: tall and dark, with the kind of cleanly hewn good looks which would appeal to any woman…

Blood rushed to her head and she swayed. What was Owen Gallagher doing here?

CHAPTER TWO

OWEN had never fully appreciated before what the saying about being pole-axed had meant, but he understood it now. It felt as though he'd been riveted to the spot as he stared at Rose Tremayne. What was *she* doing here? he wondered dazedly. However, before he could attempt to work out the answer, the doors crashed open as the next patient was rushed in.

'Bed two. Suzanne, you take charge. I'll be with you once I've checked this one out.' Owen snapped back into action, feeling his heart thundering as he strode over to the bed. He didn't look at Rose as he bent over the young man because he couldn't afford to let himself get distracted. 'What do we know so far?'

'Motorcyclist with severe injuries to both legs. GCS of ten on admission.'

It was Rose who answered, and he felt his skin prickle with awareness when he recognised the sweetly husky tones. His mouth thinned as she continued updating him on the patient's status. There was no way on earth that he was prepared to think of her as an attractive woman. She was a threat to his son and that was all there was to it.

'He needs intubating and I want another line put in, stat! And can someone get rid of those clothes? How the hell can I examine him properly when he's trussed up in those?'

He quickly set about intubating the patient, ignoring the

fact that everyone had fallen silent. So maybe it wasn't usual for him to order people around like that, but this wasn't a usual day, was it? Having Rose Tremayne turn up in his department was something he had never allowed for. He wasn't sure what she'd hoped to achieve by it, but there was no way he was letting her get anywhere near Daniel if that was what she'd been planning.

The thought of her duplicity was very hard to swallow and he swore under his breath as he eased the endoctracheal tube down the young man's throat. Rob Lomax, one of the two registrars who were on duty that day, looked at him in surprise.

'Are you OK, Owen?'

'Fine. I suggest you concentrate on what you're supposed to be doing instead of worrying about me.'

Owen ignored the looks the team exchanged at yet another example of his strange mood that day. He would make his peace with them later, after he'd calmed down—*if* he calmed down, he amended as Rose Tremayne moved around the bed and into his line of sight. What the hell was she doing here?

The only person who could answer that question was Rose herself, and there was no way he could ask her *it* at the present moment. He finished intubating while she cut away the young man's leather jacket and then carried on with his examination, logging up a couple of broken ribs as well as a dislocated shoulder.

'X-rays,' he rapped out, moving to the bottom of the bed so he could examine the man's legs, which were a mess. The right tibia was sticking through the flesh and the left foot was twisted at such an odd angle that the ligaments had to be ruptured. It was going to take the orthopaedic team several hours to put this jigsaw back together, he thought grimly as he turned to Beth Humphreys, the senior radiologist.

'Both legs need doing as well as the usual—lateral cervical spine and anteroposterior views of the chest and pelvis. And can you send a copy through to the orthopaedic department so they know what they'll be dealing with?'

He moved away after Beth had assured him that she would get straight onto it and went to see how Suzanne was faring. Although the registrar was extremely capable, she tended to doubt her own ability and needed a bit of gentle encouragement at times.

'So what have we got here?' he asked, standing beside Suzanne because it meant that he had his back to Rose Tremayne. The less he saw of her the better, he thought darkly, then deliberately erased the thought from his mind. If she'd hoped to upset him by turning up here then she was going to be disappointed.

'Jane Robinson, aged fifty-five, presented with severe chest pain. She was a rear-seat passenger in the second vehicle that crashed.' Suzanne frowned as she looped her stethoscope around her neck. 'GCS fifteen on admission. Blood gases normal for both oxygenation and acid-base status, and both lungs are clear. There's no history of cardiac problems, but there's extensive bruising down the centre of her chest.'

'Right.' Owen turned to the woman. 'I'm Owen Gallagher, the consultant in charge of the trauma unit. Were you wearing a seat belt when the accident happened?'

'Yes. My daughter insisted I should wear it… Where is she? Has she been brought in yet? I want to see her…!'

'I'll get one of the nurses to check,' he said soothingly. He looked around but everyone appeared to be busy at that moment apart from Rose. He steeled himself and beckoned her over. 'Can you find out if this lady's daughter has been admitted yet?'

'Of course.' She turned to the woman and smiled, and Owen felt his breath catch. Rose Tremayne had the most beautiful smile he'd ever seen, so warm and caring that it felt as though it could melt away any problems one might have had. It obviously had a comforting effect on Mrs Robinson because she immediately calmed down.

'Can you tell me your daughter's name?' Rose asked quietly, but he'd prepared himself and the sound of her voice caused only the most minimal reaction this time.

'Shelley…Michelle, I mean. Michelle Robinson.'

'I'll see what I can find out for you.'

Rose gave the woman's hand a gentle squeeze then hurried away. Owen breathed a sigh of relief as she left the resuscitation room. Now that she'd gone he should be able to function on all cylinders again.

It was alarming to realise the effect she had on him. He tried not to think about it as he turned to the patient. 'I need to examine you, so try not to worry. I'm sure there will be news of your daughter very shortly.'

Mrs Robinson didn't demur as he set about the familiar routine. He frowned when he saw the full extent of the bruising down the centre of her chest. 'How did this happen? I can see the marks from your seat belt, but I can't understand where you got these bruises from.'

'It was my own fault,' Jane Robinson admitted guiltily. 'Shelley told me to put it in the boot but I didn't want it getting damaged.'

'Were you holding something on your knee?' he guessed, gently exploring the area. The bruising extended from just below her collar-bones right down to her waist—following the line of her sternum, in fact. It was possible that she'd broken a rib or two but he wasn't convinced it was that which was causing her so much pain.

'Well, not on my knee, exactly. It was too heavy for that. I had it propped in the footwell in front of me.' She sighed. 'It was a table, you see, with a marble top, and I didn't want it getting chipped.'

'And when the car crashed you slammed into it?' Owen said, rapidly putting two and two together.

'Yes. There wasn't much room with the table in front of me,

so even though I was wearing my seat belt, it still rammed right into my chest…'

She broke off and gulped. Owen frowned when he saw her start struggling for breath. 'Can you tell me how severe the pain is at this moment?'

'It's really bad, Doctor, and I can't seem to breathe properly…' She suddenly stopped talking and her eyes rolled up into her head. The cardiac monitor started beeping to warn them that there was no output from her heart.

'She's in VF.' Owen turned to his registrar. 'I think it's a cardiac tamponade—the heart is being compressed because blood is collecting in the pericardium. I'll need to draw it off to relieve the pressure.'

'You think it's a fractured rib that's caused it?' Suzanne queried, hurrying round the bed.

'More likely to be the sternum. That would explain the severe pain she's been in. If the sternum has fractured, it could have pierced the pericardium, which is why there's blood collecting around her heart. She'll need to go straight to Theatre once we've finished. Shock her and give her a shot of adrenaline, but don't apply external cardiac compression—it will only make matters worse.'

He left it to Suzanne to resuscitate the woman, knowing that the registrar was perfectly capable of following his instructions. His main concern was to deal with the cause of the patient's arrest. It took him just a few moments to insert a hollow needle into the woman's chest and he nodded as he watched the blood gush back into the syringe.

'Just as I thought—cardiac tamponade. The sternum will need wiring up and the pericardium will need repairing, so the cardio team will have to crack open her chest.'

He drew off another syringe full of blood before Suzanne told him the patient's heart was beating and they had established sinus rhythm. 'Good. Get onto the cardio reg and tell him what's happened,' he instructed, peeling off his gloves. 'Make sure he understands how urgent it is. This is one occasion when queue-jumping is absolutely essential.'

Suzanne made the call, then came back to him. 'I wouldn't have known what to do if you hadn't been here. It never occurred to me that it could be a tamponade. I always associate that with a penetrating chest injury. I never considered the possibility that the sternum had fractured and pierced the pericardium even though I could see all that bruising.'

'Don't be so hard on yourself, Suzanne. There's a dozen different reasons why she could have arrested. You know that as well as I do.'

'Maybe. But you still managed to come up with the correct diagnosis.'

Suzanne looked downhearted as she went to meet the paramedics who'd arrived with another casualty. Owen made a note to have a word with her later and went to check on the young man with the leg injuries. Beth had the X-rays on the computer screen and he sighed when he saw the extent of the damage that had been done to the man's ankle.

'That's going to take some sorting out. It will be a while before he'll be able to walk on it. It causes a major problem when ligaments are torn like that.'

'What about his leg?' Rob queried, coming over to have a look. 'It's a real mess.'

'That's going to take time, too, and it will need external fixation from the look of it. The bone's in bits just here,' he explained, pointing to the screen. 'It will take several weeks to lay down new bone and the biggest problem will be to ensure that the tibia doesn't shorten in the meantime. That's why external fixation is the best option.'

He looked round when he sensed that someone was standing behind him and stiffened when he saw Rose. 'Yes?'

'Mrs Robinson's daughter is on her way in. ETA three minutes,' she told him quietly, then moved away.

Owen watched her walk over to the bed and it was all he could do not to go after her and demand to know what she was doing there. He'd barely slept since the night he'd met her in the pub. He knew that he'd handled the situation badly by offering her money, but it had been his last resort after everything else had failed. Now he had no idea what she was up to, but he couldn't accept that it was coincidence that had brought her to his department that day. She was planning something and, whatever it was it would have an impact on Daniel.

The thought of the damage she might cause was too much to deal with. Owen knew that he had to put some distance between himself and Rose Tremayne, otherwise he couldn't be held responsible for his actions. Spinning round on his heel, he strode out of the room, ignoring the startled looks from his staff as they watched him leave. He needed a couple of minutes on his own to think things through. If Rose did have a plan, he intended to be one step ahead of her!

Rose bit her lip as she watched the doors swing shut after Owen Gallagher had left. She knew he was furious about her being there but it wasn't her fault. She'd had no idea that he worked at St Anne's when she'd accepted this job, otherwise she wouldn't have taken it. Now she couldn't decide what to do. Should she go after him and explain that she hadn't intended to make life difficult for him by turning up in his department? Or would it be better if she left well alone?

'I wonder what's up with His Highness today.'

Rose summoned a smile when Rob Lomax came over to her. Instinct told her that it would be a mistake to let anyone know about her link to Owen Gallagher so she feigned ignorance. 'Do you mean Dr Gallagher?'

'Uh-huh. He's like a cat on a hot tin roof today and it isn't like him. That guy is the epitome of cool normally. Isn't that right, Suzie?'

'Isn't what right? And don't call me Suzie. You know I don't like it.'

'I know how you feel.' Rose smiled as the other registrar joined them. 'I hate it when people call me Rosie.'

Suzanne grimaced. 'Then my advice to you is to make sure that certain members of this staff are fully acquainted with your views.' She shot a speaking look at Rob, who tried to look hurt.

'Do you mean me?'

'If the cap fits…' Suzanne sniffed loftily and walked away.

Rose chuckled. 'That put you in your place, didn't it?'

'She loves me really,' Rob assured her, grinning. 'So, I know that your name is Rose but I don't know much else. How about filling me in over a cup of coffee after we finish up here?'

'Sorry, but I think I'd better stick to what I'm getting paid for.'

Rose smiled to take the sting out of her refusal, but nowadays she made a point of not getting involved with the male members of staff wherever she was sent to work. The few times she'd been out with a man in the past it had usually ended badly—her date had expected more from her than she'd been prepared to give. But she had made up her mind after Daniel had been adopted that she would never put herself in the position of being hurt like that again. It was much easier if she kept things on a strictly friendly footing.

'That makes a change,' Rob declared, unfazed by her refusal. 'Most of the agency staff seem to think they're here to socialise. Angie—that's the charge nurse—keeps threatening to padlock the staffroom door. Usually they spend more time in there drinking coffee than doing any work!'

'You must have been using the wrong agency,' she said lightly, not wanting to be drawn into a discussion about the merits—or pitfalls—of employing agency nurses. There was enough ill feeling as it was, without her encouraging people to think badly of all agency staff.

The porters arrived just then, to take the motorcyclist up to Theatre. Rose checked that his notes were up to date and handed him over, then went to help with the patient who'd been brought in. It was Michelle Robinson, the daughter of the woman who had suffered the heart attack, and she was in a very bad way.

Owen reappeared, and he and the team did all they could for her, but it was a losing battle from the outset. The young woman's injuries were just too extensive and she died thirty minutes later. Rose nodded when Angie asked her to remove all the leads and tubes before her family came to identify her. It would be distressing enough for them without them having to see all the unpleasant details.

Another couple of patients were brought into Resus, but Rose was asked to work the cubicles and didn't deal with them. She was glad of the change because dealing with the most severely injured was always harrowing. As she went to report to the triage nurse, she found herself remembering what Rob had said about Owen Gallagher's mood that day and sighed.

It didn't take a genius to work out why he was out of sorts. Seeing her there must have been as big a shock for him as it had been for her. All she could hope was that it wouldn't make a difficult situation any worse. No matter what he believed, she only had Daniel's best interests at heart, and if getting in touch with her would help Daniel then she most certainly wasn't going to refuse to see him.

The day wore on, the usual mix of high drama and the mundane. Overcrowded GP surgeries meant that a lot of people who came to the department didn't actually need to be treated there. Rose dealt with half a dozen minor injuries ranging from a deeply embedded splinter to a sore throat then, at Angie's behest, went for a break.

There were a couple of other nurses in the staffroom when she went in and she tried not to take it personally when they ignored her. She never stayed in one place long enough to make friends, so she was used to being ignored. She made herself a cup of coffee and had just sat down to drink it when the door opened and Owen Gallagher appeared.

She had managed to keep out of his way since she'd left Resus. With her working the cubicles, it hadn't been that difficult to avoid him and she'd been glad of the respite. Knowing that she was an object of loathing in his eyes wasn't the most pleasant experience she'd ever had. Now she stiffened as his gaze skimmed over the other nurses and landed on her. Even from that distance she could see the chill in his grey eyes. He strode towards her and his face was like thunder when he stopped in front of her.

'There is a waiting-room full of people out there. I suggest you attend to what you're being paid for, Ms Tremayne. And, to my knowledge, that doesn't include sitting here, drinking coffee.'

His tone was icy with contempt and Rose flushed. She didn't say a word as she got up, took her mug to the sink and emptied the coffee down the drain. Nobody said anything as she left the staffroom but she could feel the other nurses watching her and it was galling to know what they must be thinking.

They probably thought she wasn't pulling her weight after what Owen Gallagher had said, and the unfairness of being labelled as lazy was very hard to take. She did a good job wherever she worked and put one hundred per cent effort into it, too. That was why she'd been offered so many permanent posts—every hospital she'd worked at had asked her if she would like to join their staff, but she'd had to refuse.

It wasn't that she didn't like the idea of working in one place, because she would have loved to do so. It was the fact that she wouldn't earn her current salary that stopped her. As her father had sunk deeper into the grip of Alzheimer's disease she'd had to move him into a nursing-home, and the fees were extortionate. Agency work paid far more than she could earn by working for the NHS, plus she could top up her income by working nights if the nursing-home's fees increased. Maybe she should have explained all that to Owen—only what would have been the point? He wasn't interested in her problems, he was only interested in keeping her away from Daniel.

Rose went back to the unit and took a fresh file out of the tray, determined that she wouldn't give him the opportunity to accuse her of wasting time again. The waiting-room was packed and she had to shout to make herself heard above the din.

'Vicky Smith.'

A girl in her twenties stood up, clutching her left hand. Rose grimaced when she saw the state of her ring finger. 'That looks very nasty,' she said, leading the young woman to a cubicle. 'How did it happen?'

'I was bringing my horse in from the field when he tried to bolt. The lead rope must have got wrapped around my finger somehow because I heard it make this horrible popping sound.' Vicky sat down on the bed, looking very pale as she studied her swollen hand. 'Do you think it's broken?'

'It could be, but I'll have to get one of the doctors to take a look at it before we can be sure.' Rose smiled at her. 'It will probably need X-raying so there'll be a bit of wait. Did you come here on your own or did someone bring you?'

'I came on my own.' Vicky looked close to tears. 'I was going to phone my boyfriend but Oliver—that's my horse—trampled on my mobile phone and broke it.'

'I can phone him for you,' Rose assured her. She jotted down the boyfriend's phone number then went to find Suzanne and asked her to take a look at the girl's hand. As she had predicted, Suzanne wanted X-rays to be done so Rose ushered the young woman to the radiology unit and left her there while she made the telephone call. Angie was using the phone on the desk, so rather than waste time waiting until it was free Rose found some change in her pocket and used the public phone in the foyer. She was just hanging up after telling Vicky's boyfriend what had happened when Owen Gallagher came out of the department and he stopped dead when he saw her.

'I've warned you once today about getting on with your work, Ms Tremayne, and I don't intend to warn you again about flagrantly wasting time. You're paid to work, not to organise your social life.'

'Do you always speak to staff this way or have you singled me out for special treatment because of Daniel?' Rose was incensed. She had never been spoken to in such a fashion before and she refused to stand there and meekly accept it.

'This has nothing to do with my son!' Gallagher glared at her. 'I will not tolerate incompetence in any way, shape or form.'

'Of course it has to do with your son!' Rose spat the accusation back at him. 'You've got it into your head that I am a threat to Daniel's well-being and that's why you are behaving this way.'

'And can you blame me?' He took a step towards her so that, instinctively, she tried to retreat. However, with the wall at her back there was nowhere to go. Her heart began to pound as he bent and stared into her eyes. She had never seen such dislike on anyone's face before. It was all she could do to stand there as he continued in the same relentless tone when what she wanted to do was to run away and hide.

'I don't know what kind of a game you're playing, Ms Tremayne, but one thing I do know: it won't work. I won't let you ruin Daniel's life.'

'I have no intention of ruining his life,' she protested.

'No? Then what are you doing here? What exactly do you hope to achieve by harassing me?'

'I didn't know that you worked here! I was just as shocked as you were when I saw you this morning.'

'And you really expect me to believe that?' He laughed shortly, his deep voice devoid of humour. 'I'm sorry but I don't believe in coincidences, so you'll have to come up with a better story than that.'

'It's the truth! I'm here because the agency I work for sent me here. That's it. There's no other reason.'

Just for a moment a flicker of uncertainty showed in his eyes before he shook his head. 'No, it's just too convenient. You turn up in my department and expect me to believe that you didn't plan this—'

'Plan what? What possible good could it do me to come here?'

'I don't know. That's the whole point, isn't it? I have no idea what you're up to. You, Ms Tremayne, are an unknown quantity. And until I find out what you want, I am not going to be foolish enough to believe a single word you say.'

With that, he walked away. Rose took a shaky breath but her heart was hammering after the bitter attack. What made it worse was that she could sympathise with his fears. He *didn't* know her, so he had no idea what kind of person she was. Oh, she could tell him that she meant Daniel no harm but why should he believe her? She was a threat in Owen Gallagher's eyes and he was going to do everything in his power to keep her out of Daniel's life.

The thought was more painful than it should have been in view of the fact that she'd had over a week to get used to the idea. Rose wasn't sure why it upset her so much. Obviously, if there was a chance that she could get to know Daniel then she wouldn't allow anything to stop her, yet it hurt to know that Owen would hate her all the more if she flouted his wishes. She couldn't help wishing they could put aside their differences for Daniel's sake, but the likelihood of that happening was nil.

The one thing Owen Gallagher didn't want from her was friendship!

CHAPTER THREE

IT WAS the longest day of Owen's life, and he couldn't wait for it to end. Although he tried to avoid any further contact with Rose, it wasn't possible to escape from her completely. Several times he found himself working alongside her, and each time it was all he could do to hide his animosity.

The sooner she left his department, the better, he thought grimly as he went into the office to check the rosters and see who was on duty the following day. They were carrying three vacancies at the present time—two nurses and a senior registrar—so they had been relying on agency staff to fill in the gaps. As he skimmed his finger down the chart, he felt his stomach sink. Angie had pencilled in 'Agency' in the nursing column for the following three weeks and he could only hope that it wouldn't be Rose who was working for them. After all the hassle she'd caused him that day, he could do without having to spend the next three weeks working with her.

'Checking what cover we've got?'

Owen glanced round when Angie came into the office. 'Yes. I see you've hired agency staff for the next three weeks.'

'I had to.' Angie sighed as she glanced at the roster. 'Now that Maggie's gone on maternity leave we're really struggling for cover. I know it's costly to use agency staff, but I haven't any choice. And at least the agency came up trumps this time.

Rose is great, isn't she? It's wonderful to have someone who actually knows what she's doing for a change.'

'I wasn't all that impressed with her,' he said curtly, hanging the chart back on its hook. 'Not only did I catch her in the staffroom drinking coffee, but she was also using the payphone in the foyer to organise her social life.'

'Actually, I insisted she took a break.' Angie shrugged when he looked at her in surprise. 'I know what you're thinking— *I'm* usually the one banging on about the amount of work agency staff do, but Rose isn't like that. She's a really hard worker.'

'And the phone call?' Owen said cynically, not convinced.

'She could have been making the call for one of the patients. The girl who'd broken her finger asked me to thank Rose for getting in touch with her boyfriend,' Angie explained. 'I heard Rose say something about using the payphone when I was using the one in Reception, so that probably explains what she was doing.'

'I see.' Owen's mouth compressed. Maybe it was unfair of him to have assumed the worst, but Rose only had herself to blame. If she hadn't wheedled herself a place in his department, he wouldn't be a bag of nerves from wondering what she was up to.

The thought of what Ms Tremayne might be plotting was more than he could cope with at the end of such a stressful day so Owen said his goodbyes and left. It was a thirty-minute drive to his home in Richmond on a good day, but the traffic was horrendous that night. It was almost seven by the time he let himself into the house, to be greeted by the thunderous delights of rock music pounding through the ceiling.

He sighed as he hung his coat in the cloakroom and made his way upstairs. The last thing he wanted was another confrontation with Daniel about the amount of time he wasted when he should be studying. He didn't want to play the heavy-handed father all the time, but what else could he do? He couldn't take the easy route and allow his son to ruin his whole future.

Owen rapped on the bedroom door and went in. Daniel was lying on his bed, playing air guitar. There was a pile of books on his desk but there was no sign that the boy had attempted to do any work. Walking over to the socket, Owen pulled out the plug, sighing in relief when the music immediately stopped.

'*Dad!*' Daniel leapt to his feet, looking pained as he hurried to the stereo to check if one of his precious vinyls had been damaged.

'I thought we agreed that you'd cut down the amount of time you spend listening to music,' Owen said quietly, deciding it would be less stressful if he adopted a reasonable approach. He really didn't feel like getting into another argument. He'd had his fill after that last confrontation with Rose Tremayne.

The memory of what had happened still had the power to anger him but he battened down his emotions. 'Have you done that geography essay yet? It has to be handed in by the end of this week.'

'I was going to do it after dinner,' Daniel explained mutinously, taking the record off the deck and carefully stowing it away in its cardboard sleeve.

'Dinner will be a good half-hour yet, so why not make a start on it?' he suggested mildly. There was no point ordering Daniel to get it done—experience had shown that the boy would make a mess of it on purpose if he did so. Daniel reacted badly to people ordering him about—just like his mother did.

The thought sent a rush of emotions scudding through him. Owen spun round on his heel, not wanting Daniel to see how upset he was. The fact that he had automatically linked Rose to his son made him feel all sorts of things, from guilt to a mind-numbing fear. He couldn't afford to start noticing similarities in their behaviour—it was too dangerous. Rose was a stranger, and just because she had a problem with authority it didn't mean that Daniel had inherited it from her.

'I'll give you a shout when dinner is ready,' he said, going to the door.

Daniel muttered something in reply, but for once Owen wasn't listening to what his son was saying. He was too busy trying to fight his own inner demons. He went downstairs and made them a meal. And the whole time he was grilling and chopping his mind was spinning in ever-decreasing circles.

He needed to find a solution to the problem of Rose Tremayne but it wasn't going to be easy. If... He paused at that point and took a deep breath to steady himself then carried on. *If* Rose was as stubborn as Daniel, she wasn't going to go away. She wasn't going to stay quietly in the background either. Once she received Daniel's letter then she would respond to it, and no amount of threats or coercion by him would change her mind.

His main aim had been to keep her out of Daniel's life, but if it wasn't possible to do that he would have to try a different tactic. Wasn't there a saying about knowing one's enemy? It might work very well in this instance. At the moment Daniel seemed to believe that his birth mother was some wonderful almost mythical being who was imbued with goodness and grace, but once he met her, he could change his mind.

The reality couldn't possibly live up to his overly high expectations, and that was what Owen needed to concentrate on. Instead of keeping Rose away from his son, maybe he should let them meet and allow Daniel to form a true opinion of the woman who had given him away?

Just for a moment the thought flashed through his mind that perhaps his son wouldn't be disappointed, but he refused to consider it. Rose might be many things but she wasn't a saint!

Rose went straight home after she'd finished her shift. As she let herself into the building she could feel her heart racing. Ever since Owen had told her that Daniel had written to her, she had been waiting for his letter to arrive. She knew it could take some time to reach her, because it would have to be forwarded by the adoption agency. There was a system in place whereby a parent or an adopted child could leave a note in their files to say that they would welcome contact from the other party, which was how Owen had been able to get in touch with her. His letter had been forwarded by the agency, although she wouldn't have been quite so keen to follow it up if she'd had an inkling of the outcome. Why *did* he consider her such a threat?

There was no answer to that question, or none that she could come up with, at least. Closing the front door, she went straight to the mailboxes at the back of the foyer. Every flat in the block had its own mailbox on the ground floor, to save the postman having to trek upstairs. She unlocked her box and sorted through the usual collection of junk mail and bills until she came to a familiar white envelope bearing the address of the adoption agency on its back flap. Daniel's letter had arrived.

Rose made her way to the lift and stood there in a fever of impatience as it carried her up to the sixth floor. She let herself into her flat and ripped open the envelope, not bothering to read the accompanying note. She just wanted to read Daniel's letter and see what he had to say.

The letter was quite short, just a few lines written in an unsteady hand, explaining that he hoped she didn't mind him writing to her but that he would like to see her if it was possible. He'd included his address at the top and his phone number, then repeated them again at the bottom.

Rose's eyes filled with tears. Despite its brevity, she knew the effort it must have cost him to write it. Daniel had no idea if she would reply, and the thought of him sitting at home, wondering and waiting as she'd been doing, was more than she could bear. Reaching for the phone, she dialled the number, her heart pounding as she listened to it ringing, once, twice, three times…

'Owen Gallagher.'

She dropped the receiver back onto its rest. How could she have forgotten about Daniel's father and his animosity towards her? There was no way that he would allow her to speak to Daniel, so she would have to write to him instead…

The phone rang, startling her so much that she jumped. She was trembling as she picked up the receiver. 'Hello?'

'Ms Tremayne? It's Owen Gallagher. I believe you just tried to phone me.'

'H-how did you get my number?' she whispered.

'I dialled 1471.'

His tone was brisk and she winced when she realised how foolish she'd been to make such a basic error. Now that he knew Daniel's letter had reached her he would do everything in his power to keep them apart, maybe even go so far as to make sure that Daniel never received her reply

'…and that's why I've decided you two should meet.'

Rose blinked as she caught the tail end of what Gallagher was saying. 'I'm sorry, but what did you say?'

'I said that I've changed my mind and I think that you should meet Daniel. Now all we need to do is to work out a time that will be convenient—'

'Just a moment.' She took a deep breath, trying to clear the fog of panic from her head so she could think. She couldn't understand why he'd changed his mind after what he'd said to her that day. 'Why have you had a change of heart all of a sudden? You made it perfectly clear that you didn't want me to see Daniel, yet now you're offering to arrange a meeting with him. It doesn't make sense.'

'After considering all the facts, I've decided this might be the best way forward for all of us.'

'I find it very hard to believe that you're doing this for my benefit, Dr Gallagher,' she said scathingly, 'so what is really going on?'

'Nothing. I'm entitled to change my views the same as anyone else is, surely?'

Rose shivered when she felt the rich deep tones strumming across her nerves. Up till then she'd been more concerned with the content of what he'd been saying and it was only now she realised what a beautiful voice he had—and that it matched his appearance.

The thought made her gasp, and she clamped her lips together to stop any sound escaping. She couldn't afford to show any sign of weakness in front of this man. Even though he appeared to be offering her an olive branch, she wasn't convinced it was what he actually intended. Until she knew what he was up to, she had to be on her guard.

'I think it would be best if you two met somewhere Daniel feels at ease. Here, at home, might be best.'

'It would be far too stressful for him to meet me there,' Rose said quickly, setting aside her own concerns for the moment. 'It needs to be somewhere neutral—a place where he won't feel guilty.'

'Guilty?'

His tone had sharpened and she sighed. She wasn't deliberately trying to annoy him, but she'd read all the research that had been done about adopted children and how they felt when meeting their birth parents, and the biggest factor of all was the guilt they often experienced.

'Adopted children who have been brought up in a happy and loving home often feel guilty about making contact with their birth parents. They feel that they are letting their adoptive parents down and I don't want Daniel to be put in that position, do you?'

'No, I don't. So what do you suggest, Ms Tremayne?'

There was far less assurance in his voice this time and Rose felt her heart suddenly ache when she realised what he must be going through. The situation was just as difficult for him as it was for her. Her voice softened, unconsciously taking on the soothing cadence she used so often with patients who were deeply traumatised.

'I think we should ask Daniel where he would like to meet me. He is the most important person in all of this, and we need to ensure that he feels completely comfortable with the arrangements.'

'Do you want to speak to him now and ask him yourself?'

Rose couldn't think of anything she would like more than to do just that, but now that she was thinking clearly she could see how stressful it would be for the boy to have to speak to her without prior warning.

'No. It would be better if you told him that I'd phoned and gave him my telephone number. That way he can get in touch with me when he's ready.'

'Yes, you're right.' Owen paused, and it sounded as though the words were being forced out of him when he continued. 'Thank you. You've been very understanding and I appreciate it.'

Rose didn't have time to reply because he hung up. She put the receiver back in its rest, then picked up the letter and read it again. Half a dozen lines, which had bridged a gap of years and brought her precious son back into her life. All she could do now was pray that everything would work out the way she hoped it would. She didn't want to replace Daniel's mother—she couldn't even if she tried. She just wanted to be there for him if he needed her. Yet so much depended on Owen, didn't it?

He might have seemed much more reasonable tonight but she wasn't convinced he would continue to behave that way. It all depended on whether he still believed she was a threat and, quite frankly, she didn't know how to convince him that she wasn't. The only thing she could do was to be herself and hope it would be enough to reassure him.

Owen had spent another restless night, so he felt tired and out of sorts when he arrived at work the following morning. Daniel had veered between euphoria and terror when he'd found out that Rose had phoned. It had been sheer torture to watch him getting so stressed and not be able to do anything about it. It was a father's responsibility to protect his child and Owen hated feeling so powerless. The fact that he'd found his attitude towards Rose softening had troubled him, too. He couldn't afford to lower his guard.

The thought that he might have allowed himself to be taken in by her apparent concern was very hard to swallow. He was in no mood to compromise when he strode into the A and E unit so it was unfortunate that Rob was making the most of the lull between patients to chat up their new receptionist, Polly. Owen's face was like thunder as he strode over to the reception desk and tapped his registrar on the shoulder.

'If you spent less time on your love life, you might actually make something of yourself, Dr Lomax. Have you no work to do? I can soon find you something if you haven't.'

'I…um…Yes. Sorry, sir.'

Rob leapt away from the counter and disappeared towards the cubicles, leaving Owen feeling like some sort of a throwback to earlier times. He'd worked for a consultant who'd had a hair-trigger temper early on in his career and he hated to think that he was starting to exhibit the same tendencies. He sighed as he went to the office. It was wrong to allow his personal problems to intrude on his work….

'Oops!'

He ground to a halt when Rose came hurrying out of the office and cannoned right into him. There was a moment when their bodies were in the most intimate contact—breast to breast, thigh to thigh—and his heart gave an almighty lurch when he felt her soft curves nestling against him. In the two years since Laura had died he hadn't wanted another woman. He'd been celibate out of choice, not through lack of opportunity, yet all of a sudden his libido was asserting itself. He took a hasty step back when he felt his body quicken, hating the fact that it was Rose of all people who had caused this reaction.

'I'm sorry. I should have looked where I was going.' She sounded almost as shocked as he felt, and Owen felt his body respond with even more fervour to that idea. Had she experienced the same rush of desire he had? Was her body quickening, too, her senses coming alive because of his nearness?

His gaze dropped to her breasts before he could stop himself and the blood began to drum along his veins when he saw how her nipples were pressing against the thin fabric of her uniform—proof, indeed, that she'd been equally aroused by the contact. All of a sudden it felt as though the walls were closing in on him. He knew that he had to extricate himself from the situation as quickly as possible, but it appeared that Rose had other things on her mind now.

'Did you tell Daniel that I'd phoned last night?' she said quickly as he went to move away.

'Yes, I did.' Owen paused, torn between making his escape before anything else happened and carrying through with his plan. He took a deep breath and forced his rioting libido to settle down. If he was to rid himself of the threat this woman posed to his son, he had to learn how to deal with her.

'And how did he react? Was he upset? Excited? Scared?' She laughed, and there was a wealth of tenderness in her voice. 'Or all three at once, more likely!'

'He veered between euphoria and terror,' he replied shortly. So what if she sounded truly concerned—was he really going to take it at face value when he couldn't rule out the possibility that she had an ulterior motive? Nevertheless, it was hard to convince himself that she had anything except Daniel's welfare at heart when she spoke about him that way.

'Did he?' She stared at the floor for a moment and there were tears in her eyes when she looked up. 'It must be so *confusing* for him. I can't bear to think about what he's going through. I know how I feel and if it's anywhere near as—'

'I gave him your telephone number.'

Owen cut her off in mid-sentence because he really didn't want to know how she felt. Maybe it was a sign of his own weakness, but he couldn't afford to take any account of her feelings. It was Daniel who mattered, and Daniel who must be his only concern. How Rose felt wasn't an issue.

'Oh. Right. Thank you.'

Her smile was no more than the merest flicker yet he felt its effects in every cell of his body. He didn't say a word as he turned round and made his way back to Reception. Polly glanced nervously at him as he passed her desk, but he wasn't interested in tearing her off a strip for chatting to his registrar. He had too much else on his mind.

He took the stairs to the first floor two at a time and went straight to his office. He spent very little time in there because he'd always preferred a hands-on approach when it came to running the department. His maxim was to be seen *and* heard, so there was no skulking in his office for him as there was for so many consultants. However, it was the perfect place at the moment, the only place he could think of where he could get a few minutes' peace.

Sitting down behind his desk, Owen closed his eyes and tried to rid himself of all the tension that filled him. It wasn't an easy thing to do because it had been building up for years. He'd tried to remain strong when Laura had been diagnosed with cancer, knowing how important it was to have a positive attitude. Even when it had become apparent that she'd been losing the battle he'd never wavered.

After she'd died, he'd needed to be strong for Daniel, and he could honestly say that he had managed it, too. It was only when Daniel had started talking about finding his birth mother that he had found it difficult to cope. And now that he'd met Rose… *Well!*

He shot to his feet and started pacing the floor, unable to withstand the torrent of emotions that were flooding through him. Rose worried him on so many levels that it was hard to know how he really felt about her. He didn't trust her, yet couldn't explain why. It was gut instinct that had warned him to keep her out of his life, and it was gut instinct that had told him to draw her closer. It was instinct that had made him respond to her just now, too. His feelings towards her weren't based on fact, they were rooted in emotion—fear, anger, desire. And that was what scared him most of all. How could he hope to do what was right when he had no idea how to handle all these feelings she aroused inside him?

Rose felt tense and on edge all morning long. She might have attributed it to nervousness at the thought of Daniel phoning her, but she knew it wasn't just that. Bumping into Owen as she'd come out of the office had affected her in a way she would never have expected it to. She couldn't remember having experienced such a strong physical reaction to anyone before, and it alarmed her that she should have felt that way about Owen when it would only complicate matters. She had to control these unwelcome feelings and not let them get out of hand.

Fortunately, they started to get busy just before lunch so she was able to focus on work. Three teenagers had been found unconscious and ambulances had been despatched to bring them into the department. Rose immediately offered to forgo her break when Angie told her what had happened.

'Are you sure?' the charge nurse said, frowning. 'You're entitled to a meal break—it's in your contract.'

'It's probably in yours, too, but that won't stop you working,' she replied lightly.

Angie laughed. 'You're right there! Anyway, thanks. If you could cover Resus with Julie and Ellen, that would be a big help. Sharon can take her break and I can keep things ticking over out here.'

Rose nodded. She followed the nurses into Resus and made sure everything was ready when the ambulances arrived. The other women seemed a bit more approachable that day, and showed her where the various supplies were kept to save her having to hunt for them. By the time the first stretcher was wheeled in she felt as though they were starting to accept her, and she had to admit that it felt good to be part of the team for a change.

She grabbed a corner of the board and helped transfer the patient onto the bed. It was a young girl and she was unconscious. 'Where was she found?' Rose asked the paramedic.

'In her bedroom. From the look of all the bottles that were strewn around, she and her friends must have been drinking until they passed out.'

'So it's alcohol related?' Rose sighed. 'She doesn't look old enough to be drinking alcohol, does she?'

'She's fourteen, according to her parents. They start younger and younger these days,' the paramedic replied wearily as he left.

Rob arrived just then, and came over to Rose. He grimaced when she relayed what the paramedic had told her. 'Binge drinking is the scourge of modern society. Just wait until you've done a stint here on a Saturday night and then you'll get an idea what a problem it is.'

'I've seen the effects it can have when I've worked in other A and E departments,' she assured him.

'Of course you have. I keep forgetting that you travel around.' Rob grinned at her. 'You've fitted in so well here that I keep thinking you're part of our staff.'

'Thanks.' Rose smiled at him, truly appreciating the compliment. Turning away, she reached for the leads to attach the teenager to the bedside monitoring equipment and paused when she realised that Owen was watching her. There was something on his face, a kind of raw awareness, that made her long to tell him that she was just as aware of him, too…

He turned away as the next patient was rushed in, and she carried on with what she was doing—linking the girl to the machine so that her BP, heart rate and oxygen saturation levels could be monitored. It was a task she'd done countless times before, but this time she had to concentrate to make sure she did everything right.

There was no room for error in her job; people depended on her. There was no margin for error with regard to Owen Gallagher either; she had to get it right for Daniel's sake. And letting herself get carried away by the idea that Owen was interested in her would be a mistake of epic proportions. The only thing Owen was interested in was his son. She had to remember that or suffer the consequences.

CHAPTER FOUR

'SHE'LL need to be kept in under observation. Can you get onto the bed manager and see if he can find her a bed? She's only thirteen so there might be one free in Paediatrics. I'll have a word with her parents while you're doing that.'

Owen left Suzanne to make the arrangements and made his way out of resus. Of the three girls who'd been brought in, Alice Delaney was the one he was most concerned about. She was diabetic and that had exacerbated the problems caused by her binge drinking. Her glucose levels were shot to hell and it was going to take some time to stabilise her. The girl's parents were in the relatives' room so he went straight in and introduced himself.

'I'm Owen Gallagher, head of trauma care.' He sat down, seeing the worry that was etched on their faces. 'Alice is still unconscious but she's stable,' he explained, so as not to prolong their agony. 'Because her body is struggling to process the alcohol she's consumed, it's affected her glucose levels. She will need to be monitored so she will be admitted to a ward. I believe she's one of Dr Chang's patients so I've alerted him and he will take charge of her treatment after she leaves this department.'

'Oh, thank heavens!' Alice's mother put her hand over her mouth. She could barely speak because she was sobbing so hard. 'I don't know what got into her...really, I don't...'

'Is it the first time she's done something like this?' he asked, wondering if any parent could answer that question with any degree of certainty. Daniel had been through a similar episode after Laura had died—he'd gone out binge drinking. If he hadn't seen the results for himself, he wouldn't have believed his son would do something so stupid.

Fortunately, he'd managed to make Daniel see how foolish it was, but his biggest fear was that the boy would lapse back into the same kind of behaviour if he was put under too much pressure. That was one of the main reasons why he'd been so loath to allow any contact to take place between Daniel and Rose.

'No, it isn't the first time, Dr Gallagher. She's done it before—several times, in fact.' Alice's father shook his head when his wife tried to intervene. 'There's no point you trying to cover up for her, Mary. You know as well as I do that she's been drinking. It's just good luck that she never got herself into this state before.'

'There's a lot of under-age drinking going on,' Owen said neutrally, not wanting to get embroiled in a family argument. 'Kids of Alice's age are often pressurised by their peers to join in, and it's difficult to make them understand the damage they are doing to themselves. The problem is much worse in your daughter's case, of course. If she's drinking alcopops, for instance, the high sugar content in the drinks will immediately upset the balance between her insulin and glucose levels.'

'She hates being diabetic,' Mary said in a quavering voice. 'She doesn't want her friends thinking that she's different to them. I think that's part of the reason why she went along with them when they started buying alcohol.'

'Peer pressure is very hard to withstand when you're Alice's age,' he agreed. 'My son is eighteen and I know that his friends have a far bigger influence on him than I do.'

'So what do we do, Dr Gallagher?' Mr Delaney sounded distraught. 'Alice is making herself ill because she wants people to treat her the same as everyone else.'

'Have you thought of asking her school for help? I don't mean they should single Alice out, but if the teacher could explain what diabetes is during a biology lesson, for instance, maybe her friends would accept her condition. Once the pressure to fit in is taken off her, maybe Alice will realise how silly she is to risk her health this way.'

'It's an idea, isn't it, Mary?' Mr Delaney looked at his wife. 'We'll try anything if there's a chance that it will help Alice.' He stood up and offered Owen his hand. 'Thank you, Dr Gallagher. At least you've given us something to think about and that has to be a good thing.'

'I just hope it will help.'

Owen shook hands, then went to see how Suzanne had fared in her quest for a bed. She'd managed to find one in Paediatrics so he asked her to phone for a porter then tell Alice's parents where she was being moved to. By the time everything was organised the other two girls had been moved out of Resus. One was being kept in the observation ward until the effects of the alcohol had worn off, but the other girl was well enough to be sent home with her parents. After that, it was time to attend to the rest of patients who were waiting to be seen.

He left Resus, but before he'd gone more than a couple of steps Angie waylaid him. 'RTA on its way. ETA three minutes. Do you want to take it or shall I ask Suzanne to deal with it?'

'Suzanne's just gone to tell Alice Delaney's parents where she's being moved to. Where's Rob got to?'

'He's in cubicle three with a toddler who's eaten some of his mum's iron tablets.' Angie wiped Alice Delaney's name off the whiteboard and wrote 'RTA' in the space allotted for Resus. The patient's details—name, date of birth and time of arrival—would be added later.

'In that case, I'll take it.'

Owen headed back to Resus. Rose was still there, clearing

up, and he nodded to her, doing his best to behave naturally around her. 'RTA on its way. Should be here any minute now.'

'I'll just get this tidied away so we have a clear run,' she said quietly.

She worked quickly and efficiently as she set everything to rights, her actions obviously honed by long practice, and he couldn't help being intrigued. She was a highly experienced nurse and he found himself wondering why she was doing agency work. Somehow the thought must have translated itself into speech, because the next thing he knew he was asking her.

'How come you're working as an agency nurse when departments like this one are crying out for skilled staff? Have you never wanted to further your career?'

'Yes. In fact, I was a senior charge nurse at Hope Hospital until a few years ago.'

'So why did you give it up?' he asked curiously. He saw a flicker of something cross her face but it disappeared before he could decide if it had been regret that he'd seen.

'I needed more flexible working hours. When you're in charge of a team of nurses you can't just take time off at the drop of a hat, so I resigned and started working for an agency.'

'Flexible working hours?'

He frowned as he considered what she'd said. Most NHS staff got used to shift work very early in their careers, and if they didn't they usually left the job. The fact that Rose had stuck it out long enough to reach a senior position pointed towards only one thing: her home circumstances had changed.

His heart suddenly sank. He couldn't believe that he had never considered the fact that she might have a family. He'd been so worried about the effect she might have on Daniel if she met him that he had never thought about her having other children. He couldn't begin to imagine how Daniel would feel if he found out that he had half-siblings.

'I had family responsibilities and needed to be able to choose the hours I worked.'

Family responsibilities. That had to mean children, he thought in despair. A son or a daughter—possibly both. It would break Daniel's heart if he discovered that while *he'd* been given up for adoption his half-siblings had enjoyed all their mother's love and attention.

'So this time you decided to put your children first?' His tone was scathing but he couldn't help it. Maybe it was wrong to berate her when he knew nothing about the circumstances surrounding her decision to have Daniel adopted, but he couldn't bear to think of his son's pain.

'Children?'

'You just said that you'd resigned because you had family responsibilities,' he reminded her sharply. 'Obviously you must have children—'

'I don't.' She cut him off before he could finish speaking. 'I was referring to my father. He was taken ill and I needed to care for him.'

She didn't say anything else as she went to fetch some more dressings from the cupboard. Owen watched her cross the room and the very stiffness of her posture made him suddenly ache deep inside. Why did he know that she'd been hurt by what he'd said? Why did he care?

He had no idea. But it left him feeling very mixed up to discover that he hated causing her any pain.

Rose did her best to behave as though nothing had happened, but Owen's comments had touched a raw nerve. She would have dearly loved a family of her own to love and cherish, but how could she have had another child after giving Daniel away? Maybe she hadn't had a choice at the time, and maybe she had done it with her son's best interests at heart, but the guilt and pain of losing Daniel had never gone away. She didn't deserve to have any more children when she hadn't been able to look after her son!

Pain flashed through her at the thought, but she'd become adept at battening it down. When the patient arrived she went through the drill with her usual efficiency. BP, pulse and sats levels were recorded, saline infusion replaced. Drugs were fetched and dosages checked; each and every instruction carried out to the letter. By the time the patient was stable enough to be sent to a ward she was confident that she had fulfilled her role. She was a good nurse and nobody had ever faulted her work. However, it was poor consolation to know that her professional life was a success when her personal life left such a lot to be desired.

'Thank you, everyone.' Owen glanced around the group of people who had just spent the last forty minutes saving a man's life. 'You all did a great job.'

Rose stiffened as she waited for his gaze to arrive at her, but at the very last second he turned away. She knew it had been done deliberately and it hurt to see the actual proof of how he felt about her. She wasn't worth even a passing glance, it seemed.

'You are worth your weight in gold!' Angie came bustling over to her, unwittingly picking up on the thought. 'I take back everything I've ever said about agency nurses. Some of them actually do know what they're doing!'

'Thanks.' Rose drummed up a laugh but it was painful to know that Owen thought so badly of her. Out of the corner of her eye she saw him leave Resus, and suddenly knew that she needed to have this out with him. No matter what he believed, she deserved to be given a chance to prove herself.

'In that case, would you mind if I just popped out for five minutes?' she asked, turning to Angie.

'Of course I don't mind.' Angie shooed her towards the door. 'I owe you for your lunch-hour, so you're entitled to take a break.'

'Thanks.'

Rose didn't bother explaining that she wasn't taking a break—it was too complicated. She hurried to the door, but even so she couldn't see any sign of Owen in the corridor. She went to the reception desk and asked Polly if she knew where he'd gone.

'He could be in his office.' The receptionist pointed to the gallery. 'First door on the left when you get to the top of the stairs, but be warned—he's not in the best of moods.'

'Tell me about it,' Rose said dryly, turning to hurry up the stairs. She made her way along the gallery and paused outside the office to summon up her courage then knocked on the door.

'Come in.'

Rose went in, wondering if she was mad even to consider talking to him. However, deep down she knew that they needed to resolve this issue so that any ill-feeling between them wouldn't affect Daniel. Owen was judging her by some misplaced rules of his own making and it wasn't fair!

'Can I have a word with you?' she said politely, when he glanced up.

'What about?'

His tone was blunt and she felt herself bridle. 'About your attitude towards me for starters. I have no idea why you dislike me—'

'I have no feelings whatsoever about you, Ms Tremayne.'

He leant back in his chair and studied her from under lowered lids. He'd taken off his jacket and he looked big and commanding as he sat there in his shirtsleeves, staring her down. However, if he hoped to intimidate her it wasn't going to work.

'Really?' She laughed scathingly. 'That's not how it appears to me.'

'Then maybe you should learn to toughen up. Now, if that's all—'

'It isn't.' She walked to the desk. 'No matter what you claim, you have a problem with me. I don't know why and I don't want to know either. The only thing I'm concerned about is the effect it might have on Daniel if he sees you reacting so negatively towards me.'

'I have already agreed that you can meet him, haven't I?' He stared back at her, his grey eyes the colour of steel and just as warm. 'What more do you expect? That I'm going to give you a glowing endorsement?'

'No, I don't expect that to happen. All I want is for you to allow Daniel to make up his own mind about me.' She shrugged, not wanting him to know how difficult it was for her to admit her fears. 'He might take an instant dislike to me—I really don't know. But he deserves the chance to decide on his own how he feels, without you trying to influence him.'

'I'm willing to accept that so long as you agree to play by the same rules.'

'What do you mean?'

'That you don't try to exert undue influence over him either.' He stood up abruptly so that she took an instinctive step back before she made herself stand perfectly still.

'I can't imagine how I could exert any influence over him,' she said as calmly as she could, although it was unnerving to have him looming over her. He was very tall and powerfully built, too, and she was suddenly aware of both those things in a way she shouldn't have been. Heat flashed through her veins and she held herself rigid so she wouldn't give herself away. Owen might be a very attractive man, but this wasn't the right time to be thinking about it.

'No? Then let me lay it on the line for you. He's recently lost his mother and he's still trying to come to terms with her death. That makes him extremely vulnerable to outside influences.'

'You're worried in case I try to replace your wife in Daniel's affections?' She shook her head. 'That isn't going to happen.'

'I'm worried in case you upset him at a time when he needs to remain focused.'

He didn't answer her question, yet Rose knew that it was the source of his animosity towards her. He was afraid that Daniel would transfer his affections to her, and that she would let Daniel down.

'I would never hurt him,' she said urgently. 'I just want to help him any way I can.'

'A noble sentiment, indeed—if it's true.'

'Of course it's true! Why would I say it if I didn't mean it?'

'I have no idea.' He came around the desk and stood in front of her. 'I have no idea what your motives are, Rose, but I do know that I won't allow you to use Daniel for your own ends.'

'I don't have any *motives*! I just want to get to know him.'

'Then you and I won't have a problem. Now, if you'll excuse me, I have work to do.'

He strode past her and opened the door. Rose wasn't sure what to do. She knew the problem hadn't been resolved, but what else could she say to convince him that she was genuinely concerned about Daniel?

She left the office and made her way downstairs. Angie was coming along the corridor and she stopped to wait for her. 'Been up to the canteen for something to eat?'

'I…um…I was really hungry,' Rose hedged, not wanting to tell an outright lie. Despite what Owen seemed to think, she wasn't devious by nature. Her only concern was Daniel's welfare, although convincing Owen that it was all she cared about was an uphill struggle.

'What did you have? Not that there's ever much left at this time of the day,' Angie said cheerfully, oblivious to the tumult of thoughts that were rushing around inside her head.

'Oh, nothing exciting,' she replied ambiguously, then swung round when the doors burst open and a young woman rushed in. She was carrying a little girl in her arms and it was immediately apparent that the child was having difficulty breathing.

'You take the child and I'll call Owen,' Angie instructed, thankfully forgetting about their conversation in the heat of the moment.

Rose ran over to the woman and lifted the child out of her arms. 'What happened?' she asked as she led her into the nearest empty cubicle.

'I don't know! She was colouring when all of a sudden she started choking…'

'Was she eating anything at the time—sweets or fruit, anything at all?' Rose demanded, carrying the limp little body over to the couch. The child was unconscious, her lips blue-tinged because of the lack of oxygen that was reaching her lungs.

'No, no! She was just kneeling on the floor, doing some colouring. I'd bought her some new felt-tipped pens this morning…' The woman broke off, tears welling in her eyes as she looked at the little girl.

Rose laid the child on the couch and opened her mouth so she could check for an obstruction. 'Did the pens have caps on them?'

'Caps? Why, yes, of course they did.' The woman gasped. 'I saw Lucy pulling one of the caps off with her teeth, but I told her not to do it again!'

'But she might have forgotten.' Rose placed the heel of her hand slightly above the child's navel but made sure it was well below her ribcage. Placing her other hand over the top, she pressed down with a quick upward thrust.

'What are you doing?' the mother cried in alarm.

'If she's swallowed one of the caps off those pens it could be blocking her airway and I need to dislodge it.'

She repeated the manoeuvre, then did it a third time, smiling in relief when the little girl coughed and something shot out of her mouth. Bending down, she picked up a white plastic pen top. 'Here's the culprit.'

She dropped the cap into a dish then unhooked the oxygen mask and gently placed it over the child's nose and mouth.

'You're all right now, poppet,' she said, stroking the little girl's hair. 'Just breathe through this mask for me—that's a good girl.'

'Everything all right in here?'

Rose glanced round when she heard Owen's voice. 'She'd swallowed the cap off a felt-tipped pen, but it's out now,' she explained as calmly as she could. It wasn't easy when the memory of what he'd said to her was still so fresh in her mind, but she refused to allow their personal differences to interfere with their work.

'Good. I'll just check her over and make sure she's all right.'

Rose moved aside as he approached the bed and waited while he examined Lucy. 'Everything appears to be fine,' he concluded, turning to the child's mother. 'I'd like to keep her here until she's calmed down, but you can take her home after that.'

'Thank you so much!' The woman turned to Rose. 'I don't know how to thank you for what you did just now. If you hadn't been so quick—' She broke off and shuddered. 'I'll never forgive myself for not being more careful.'

'You mustn't blame yourself,' Rose assured her. 'It's amazing what children manage to swallow or poke down their ears or up their noses.'

'You need eyes in the back of your head when you're a parent, don't you?' The woman managed a wan smile. 'Do you have any children? If you do, I'm sure you know what I mean.'

'I have a son,' Rose said quietly. It was instinct that made her look at Owen then, and her breath caught when her gaze meshed with his. Something passed between them, a feeling of connection that she had never expected. For the past eighteen years he had loved and cherished the child she had given birth to and that had forged a bond between them even if it wasn't what either of them would have chosen to happen.

All of a sudden her heart began to race as the full impact of that thought sank in. There was a link between her and Owen which could never be broken.

* * *

Owen could feel a pounding in his head but he fought against it. He couldn't bear to think that Rose had experienced the same feeling of connection, yet he knew that she had. He summoned a smile as he turned to the child's mother but it was an effort to focus when his life seemed to be falling apart around him.

'You'll need to give your daughter's details to our receptionist for our records before you leave.'

'Of course. And thank you again, Doctor.'

'My pleasure.'

One more smile, then he was free to leave, and he did. He made his way to the office, relieved to find it was empty for once. He needed time to get himself together before he spoke to anyone, time to rid himself of the thought that there might be some sort of a *bond* between himself and Rose.

He swore under his breath. The idea was ridiculous. The only thing they had in common was Daniel. They weren't kindred spirits, former lovers or even proper work colleagues, for that matter. Rose's advent into his life would be a temporary one if he had his way, their relationship as fleeting as ships that passed in the night. So why did he feel so on edge? Why did he feel as though he was on the verge of something momentous happening? Was it fear of the havoc she could cause for his son? Or fear of the damage she might do to his own life? After all, if she took Daniel away from him what would he have left?

Owen felt a cold chill envelop him as all his fears suddenly crystallised. He'd told himself that his only concern was for Daniel, but wasn't he equally concerned about what he would do if he lost the one person who made his life mean anything? Losing Laura had been a devastating blow. He'd only coped because he'd had Daniel to look after. But how would he manage if the boy transferred his affections from him to Rose?

It could happen very easily, too. After all, he was the one who constantly nagged Daniel to get his college work done, the one who curtailed his fun. It was different for Rose, though. She didn't have to impose all those boring rules because she wasn't responsible for looking after Daniel. She could involve herself in all the good things that happened in Daniel's life and leave him to deal with the rest.

Even if she didn't set out to use the situation to her advantage, it was bound to have a negative effect on his relationship with Daniel if his son compared him to Rose and she kept coming out on top. The thought of how empty his life would be if Daniel grew apart from him was more than he could bear. Rose was an even bigger threat than he'd realised, and he had to find a way to minimise the risk she posed to him as well as to Daniel. And the only way he could do that was by getting to know her better. There was a saying about keeping your friends close and your enemies closer, so that was what he must do.

Rose was glad when it was time to go home. What had happened in the cubicle had shaken her. When Rob asked her if she wanted to go for a drink with the staff after work, she made an excuse. She just wanted to go home and think about what had gone on between her and Owen.

She left the hospital and hurried to the bus stop, but three buses drove past without stopping, all packed with commuters. She had just settled down to wait for the next one when she saw a car slow down, and her heart leapt in alarm when she realised it was Owen's car. He pulled up beside the kerb and rolled down the window.

'Hop in and I'll give you a lift.'

'There's no need,' she said quickly, because the last thing she needed was to spend any more time with him.

'I want to talk to you, so please get in.'

Short of making a scene, Rose couldn't think what else she could do. Opening the car door, she slid into the seat.

'Fasten your seat belt.'

Her mouth compressed as she buckled the seat belt across

her. If his tone was any indication of his mood they weren't going to get very far. Did he have to order her about like that?

She didn't say a word as they drove away from the hospital, determined that she wasn't going to break the silence first. If he had something to say then let him get on with it. The traffic was horrendous and they slowed to a crawl when they reached the junction with Euston Road. Owen sighed as he inched the powerful car forward.

'London is going to be gridlocked soon. In another couple of years they'll have to put a total ban on any cars entering the city.'

'The congestion charge has helped a bit,' she observed neutrally.

'It did in the beginning, but everything is going back to normal now.' He glanced at her. 'Do you drive?'

'Yes, although I don't have a car. It's too expensive to keep one on the road so I make do with public transport.'

'I try to use public transport whenever I can but it's hopeless when I'm on call. And ferrying Daniel about would be a nightmare if I didn't have a car. Like most parents of a teenager, I act as unpaid chauffeur!'

'What are his hobbies?' she asked impulsively, unable to resist finding out more about her son. 'Does he like sport?'

'Basketball is his favourite sport.' They crawled forward another couple of inches then stopped again. 'He plays for his college team and he's quite good, too. However, his main passion is music. He's into heavy metal with a vengeance!'

Rose laughed at the rueful note in his voice. 'You aren't a fan, I take it?'

'I value my hearing too much.' He flicked her a smile and she felt a flurry of heat run through her. She had to force herself to concentrate as he continued in the same, surprisingly relaxed manner.

'He also plays guitar—very badly, I might add. He and his friends have a band…or should that be a group? He's always telling me that you don't call it such-and-such a thing nowadays, but I can never remember which one I'm supposed to use.'

'One of the drawbacks of getting older,' she observed lightly, and he groaned.

'Not you as well! To hear Daniel talk, you'd think I was one step away from the knacker's yard. I used to think I was quite *with it* until he became a teenager.'

'The generation gap. I can remember thinking that my parents had no idea what life was all about too.'

'You must have been around Daniel's age when you had him,' he said quietly.

'I was a bit younger actually—just seventeen.'

She bit her lip at the painful tug of memory. She'd been so young and so naïve. If she'd been more worldly-wise, she might never have had Daniel and it was a strange feeling to know that Owen's life as well as her own could have turned out very differently if she hadn't had a baby. They might never have met, for starters, and she wasn't sure how she felt about the idea. Despite everything that had happened, she couldn't put her hand on her heart and swear that she wished she'd never met him, funnily enough.

She looked up in surprise when he suddenly steered the car out of the queue of traffic. 'What are you doing? I live in Camden, so we need to go along here.'

'I know, but we could be stuck here for ages while we wait for this traffic to clear.' He inched the car around a lorry, then glanced at her. 'We may as well find somewhere to have a drink until the worst of it has cleared.'

'Why?' She shrugged when he looked at her in surprise. 'I'm sorry, but I just don't understand what you hope to achieve by all this. Offering to drive me home, chatting about Daniel— what's in it for you, Owen?'

'I thought it might help if I made an effort to get to know you better.'

'For Daniel's sake, do you mean?'

'Yes.'

He didn't say anything else as he concentrated on getting them out of the traffic jam. Rose sank back in her seat, wondering if she was mad to go along with him. Yet what else could she do? She could hardly refuse to talk to him when it would only confirm all his suspicions about her. She had nothing to hide, so if it helped to ease the situation it had to be a good thing. Maybe he would feel better once he was sure that she meant Daniel no harm?

The thought should have reassured her, but it didn't. For some reason she couldn't explain she knew it would be a mistake to get too involved with him. Owen's only interest in her was as the mother of his son. There was no point hoping that he wanted to get to know her better for any other reason.

CHAPTER FIVE

'WHAT would you like to drink?'

Owen waited while Rose sat down. He'd driven them to Hampstead in the end, and had stopped at one of the wine bars overlooking the heath. It was the beginning of April and the evening was unusually warm, so he'd found them a table outside. There were a lot of people about—exercising their dogs or jogging—although the regular evening crowd that frequented the bar hadn't arrived yet so they had the place to themselves. It was the perfect spot to talk.

His heart seemed to leap right up into his throat at the thought of spending the next hour learning more about her. He wasn't sure why the idea alarmed him so much when he'd already decided it was the best thing to do. He fixed a smile into place, determined that he wasn't going to betray any hint of nervousness. 'How about a glass of wine?'

'That would be lovely, but could you make it a white wine spritzer, please? I worked through my lunch-break so I'd better water down the alcohol.'

'Would you like something to eat as well?' he asked, frowning in consternation.

'No, it's fine. I'll make myself some supper when I get home. Don't worry—I won't let the alcohol go to my head and disgrace myself!'

'I'm sure you won't,' he said shortly, disliking the fact that she'd felt it necessary to give him an assurance about her behaviour. As he went inside, he found himself wondering if he really did come across as so overbearing, then wondered again why it mattered. What difference did it make what she thought of him?

It was impossible to answer that question, so he put it out of his mind while he ordered a white wine spritzer for her and a glass of fresh orange juice for himself. The waitress told him she would bring their drinks to them, so he went back outside and sat down.

'The drinks will be here shortly,' he explained, settling himself more comfortably on the spindly metal chair.

'Great.' Rose picked up a cardboard coaster and started to peel away the top layer. 'Do you come here a lot?'

'To this wine bar, you mean?' He shrugged when she nodded. 'It's the first time I've been here. In fact, the last time I came to Hampstead Heath was when Daniel was about twelve. He was going through a craze for flying kites and I used to bring him here because there weren't any really big open spaces where we lived at the time.'

'Where do you live now?'

'Richmond. We moved there just before Laura found out she had breast cancer.'

'It must have been a very difficult time for you,' she said quietly.

'It was,' he said tersely, because they weren't here to discuss *his* life. He wanted to find out more about her, so he would be better prepared to deal with any problems that might arise in the future. However, before he could return the conversation to its proper track, she carried on.

'How did Daniel cope with your wife's illness? It must have hit him very hard.'

'It did.' He wasn't sure if he wanted to discuss Daniel's

problems either, but it was difficult to avoid giving her an answer. 'Laura was really brave from the moment she found the lump in her breast. She insisted that we shouldn't tell Daniel because she didn't want him worrying.'

'It must have been very stressful for you, having to keep it from him,' she said, frowning.

'We felt it was the right thing to do.'

He glanced up in relief when the waitress arrived with their drinks, not wanting Rose to see that her comment had struck a chord. Although he had respected Laura's wishes to shield Daniel for as long as possible, he had often wondered if it had made the situation more difficult for him in the end. Daniel had had less time to come to terms with what had been happening so that Laura's death had had an even bigger impact on him because of that.

'Mmm, delicious.'

He dragged his mind back to the present, summoning a smile as he picked up his own glass. 'It's not too strong?'

'No, it's fine. Thank you.' She took another sip of her drink, then put her glass on the table. 'How long ago did your wife die?'

'It will be two years this summer.'

'So Daniel would have been sixteen?'

'Yes. He was in the middle of his exams and he went to pieces. He failed most of the papers and had to resit them.'

'It was only to be expected, though. I mean, losing his mother must have been devastating for him, so it's no wonder he made a mess of his exams.'

'If it had been just his exams, it wouldn't have been so bad, but unfortunately his behaviour also changed. He got in with a bad crowd and started drinking. The crunch came when he rolled into school one day, still drunk.'

'Did you realise what was happening?'

'Yes, but I couldn't seem to get through to him. I tried everything I could think of—laid down the law, grounded him, stopped his allowance—and it didn't work. He was spiralling out of control and I was terrified he was going to end up ruining his life if he didn't get a grip.'

'So what did you do in the end?'

'I arranged for him to see a counsellor. Oh, he didn't want to go, and we had endless fights about it, but I insisted. Fortunately, it seemed to help, but I'm very aware that he's still extremely vulnerable.'

'Which is why you wanted to keep me away from him.' She picked up her glass, then put it down again, and he could see the urgency in her eyes when she looked at him. 'I give you my word that I won't do anything to upset him. I know you'll find it hard to believe this, but I really care about him, too.'

'But you don't even know him, so how can you promise not to upset him?'

It was impossible to hide his scepticism and he saw her flinch. Even though it didn't give him any pleasure, he felt duty bound to press home his point. 'You gave him away when he was a baby. You weren't there when he was growing up so you have no idea how he thinks or feels about anything. He's a stranger to you, Rose, and despite all your professed good intentions you could do exactly what you claim not to want to do. You could end up ruining his life, and that is something I will not allow you to do.'

'And *you* could ruin his life if you insist on me not seeing him.' She stared back at him, equally determined to press home her point, it seemed. 'Daniel has a right to meet me, and there is nothing you can do to stop it happening.'

'Maybe there is nothing I can do about it. But one thing I can do is promise you that you will regret it if you hurt him. He's my son, and I shall do whatever it takes to make sure he is safe and happy.'

'Then it appears we agree on something at least.' Pushing back her chair, she stood up. 'I'd like to go home now, if you don't mind.'

'Of course.'

Owen rose as well, feeling like the world's biggest louse when he saw the tears in her eyes. He'd obviously upset her with his unrelenting attitude, but her feelings weren't his main concern. It was Daniel who mattered, he reminded himself as he followed her back to the car. And Daniel whose interests he would protect above anyone else's. However, as he started the car, he could derive no satisfaction from what had happened. He might have convinced Rose that he was deadly serious about protecting Daniel, but it had come at a price. Hurting her, somehow, had hurt him far more.

Rose felt completely drained as she let herself into her flat after her meeting with Owen. She just didn't know how to convince him that she would never hurt Daniel, and it was frustrating to find herself cast in the role of villain when she'd done nothing wrong.

She made herself a sandwich and took it into the sitting room. She wasn't really hungry, but she couldn't go all day without eating anything. She turned on the television, but she couldn't seem to concentrate on the programme. She kept remembering the look on Owen's face when he'd spoken about Daniel, the way he'd seemed to believe that she was a threat to the boy's well-being. Was he right? Would it be better if she didn't meet Daniel? Even though her heart ached at the thought, she had to consider it. She would never do anything that might harm her precious child.

The phone rang and she lowered the volume on the television before picking up the receiver. 'Hello?'

'Is that Rose Tremayne?'

Rose's heartbeat quickened. Even though they'd never spoken before, she knew it was Daniel. Just for a second she wondered what she should do—should she tell him that Rose Tremayne wasn't there? It was what Owen would want her to do…

'Hello? Are you there?'

The panic in the boy's voice tugged at her heartstrings and she knew that she couldn't do it. 'Yes, I'm here. I'm Rose Tremayne.'

'I…um…I'm Daniel.'

'Hello, Daniel.' Rose took a deep breath but it was an emotional moment for both of them. 'How are you?'

'I'm OK. How about you?'

A rush of tenderness engulfed her when she heard the wobble in his voice. Despite his attempts to appear grown up and in control of himself, she knew how scary it must be for him to have to speak to her.

'I'm fine,' she said softly. 'Even better now that you've phoned me. I was hoping that you would.'

'Dad told me that you'd phoned after you'd got my letter. I want to meet you, if that's all right with you.'

'I want to meet you, too,' she replied honestly. 'When would be the best time? I expect you're in college during the week, so how about if we make it this Saturday? Would that suit you?'

'Cool! Oh, I don't know where you live, though,' he added uncertainly.

'I live in Camden, so we could meet in the centre of London if you like. How about the café in Hyde Park—the one near the end of the Serpentine? Do you know where I mean?'

'Yes! That would be great. What time?'

'Eleven o'clock?'

Daniel eagerly agreed, then said goodbye and hung up. Rose slowly replaced the receiver. She had no idea what Owen was going to say when he found out about their arrangements but she would worry about that later. For now it was enough to know that she was going to meet her son at last.

Owen tried not to overreact when Daniel told him over dinner that he had arranged to meet Rose at the weekend, but it was very difficult to behave calmly. He knew that he'd wasted his chance to get to know her better and blamed himself for getting sidetracked. He should have stuck to his guns and found out all he could about her instead of telling her so much about himself and Laura.

By the time he arrived at work the following morning he was seriously wishing that he'd never taken Rose out for that drink. It seemed to him that she had the advantage now, and it was the last thing he wanted. It didn't help that she was the first person he saw when he went into the building either.

He bade her a cool good morning and received an equally cool one in return, but the encounter unnerved him even more. He couldn't seem to escape from her. He'd dreamt about her last night—odd, disturbing dreams he didn't want to remember—and now he was going to have to spend the next eight hours working with her. Slowly but surely Rose Tremayne was taking over his life and he didn't like it one little bit!

There were only a few people waiting to be seen, so he took himself off to his office to catch up with some very overdue paperwork. He'd just signed off the previous month's statistics when his phone went and one of the nurses informed him they had received a report about a major incident that had occurred in the city. Owen hurried downstairs to find out what had happened. Angie was off duty that day and Charlie Rogers—her opposite number—was in charge of the department.

'What do we know so far?'

'Problems in that new section of the tube that's being constructed,' Charlie explained. 'That's all we know at the moment. I'm waiting for the incident control centre to get back to me.'

'Any idea of the number of casualties yet?'

'No, but it doesn't sound too good—' Charlie broke off when the phone rang. Owen waited impatiently while the

charge nurse wrote down the information that was being relayed to him.

'Well?' he snapped as soon as Charlie hung up.

'Approximately twenty known casualties so far, but there
could be more. Apparently a section of the roof caved in and
buried the men while they were working. A gas main has fractured as well, causing an explosion above ground, so that's why
they've declared it a major incident. They want us to respond
as part of the first team.'

'Right. How many staff are on duty in here today?'

'Ten including you, Rob, Suzanne and that new houseman,
Devinder,' Charlie told him.

'I'll take Rob with me. Suzanne and Devinder can cover at
this end. We'll need two nurses as well, so can I leave it to you
to organise who'll be going? Just make sure they know what
they're doing, will you? I won't have time to play nursemaid
when we get there.'

He left Charlie to sort out the arrangements and hurried to
the storeroom where they kept the protective clothing they used
for situations like this. St Anne's was part of the city's major
incident support team and they'd all been trained in the use of
the various pieces of equipment—breathing apparatus, gas
masks, decontamination suits.

He unhooked an orange coverall off its peg and pulled it on.
The garment was rather bulky, but it was designed to be wa-
terproof and to provide some level of protection in case of a
non-hazardous chemical spillage. A white hard hat was another essential in view of where they would be working. He'd
just finished kitting himself out when the rest of the team arrived and he frowned when he saw that Rose was one of the
nurses Charlie had selected to go with them.

He drew her aside, not wanting to create a fuss in front of
the others. 'Are you sure you're up to this? You're agency staff,
so you don't have to go along.'

'I'm a volunteer with the city's major incident support team so I know what I'm doing. I've done all the training and I know how to use all the equipment.'

'Fine.' He didn't waste time arguing about the rights and wrongs of her being on their team. There wasn't time when they were needed on site. He clapped his hands to gain everyone's attention.

'Once we get to the accident site you could find that you're working with staff from other hospitals. If that happens, just follow the normal procedures that have been laid down and report to your particular section leader.'

Everyone nodded to show they understood, then they left the building via the rear exit. The paramedics were waiting in the courtyard for them, so they split into two groups and got into the ambulances. Owen found himself in the same ambulance as Rose and another nurse, Pete Davenport. It was Pete's first major incident and he was very excited about it.

'Will we be going into the tunnel, do you think?' Pete demanded, leaning forward in his seat.

'It depends on what they decide to do with each team,' Owen explained calmly. 'We could be working in the tunnel or we could be above ground, attending to the casualties who were injured in the gas explosion.'

'I hope we aren't stuck outside,' Pete said in disgust. 'It would be so typical, though. My first major shout and I'll end up holding someone's hand while the rest of the guys get to do all the dangerous stuff!'

'They worked in relays the last time I was involved in an incident like this,' Rose said quietly. 'Some teams stayed outside ground zero and attended to the casualties and then after a couple of hours we swapped over.'

'Really?' Pete sounded impressed. 'So you've been on one of these little jaunts before, have you?'

'A train crash a couple of years ago,' she explained evenly.

However, Owen saw the expression that crossed her face and knew the memory wasn't a pleasant one. One of the paramedics asked Pete a question at that point, so he took advantage of the fact that the other man's attention had been diverted.

'You don't have to do this, Rose. Nobody will think any the worse of you if you decide to return to the hospital.'

'Maybe they won't, but I'll feel as though I'm letting the side down.'

'Fair enough.' He shrugged, sensing it would be a waste of time trying to persuade her. 'Was it bad...the train crash, I mean?'

'Horrendous.'

She didn't elaborate, certainly didn't attempt to turn it into a bid for sympathy, and maybe it was that which moved him most of all. Reaching out, he covered her hand with his. It was only when he felt her fingers curl around his—so small and slender yet surprisingly strong—that he realised what he was doing.

Heat rushed through him as he hurriedly let her go. He didn't look at her again as they drove along the road with the siren blaring. He didn't dare. He wasn't one hundred per cent certain what she might have seen on his face and he couldn't afford to lower his guard in any way.

Rose was the enemy.

He made himself repeat the mantra half a dozen times, but there was no weight to it, no substance. Thinking of Rose as his adversary was becoming an increasingly difficult thing to do.

The police had cordoned off the streets around the entrance to the new tunnel. Emergency service crews were arriving from all across the city and there was pandemonium as vehicles jostled for parking spaces. Owen told his team to wait with the ambulances and went to find whoever was in charge of the scene. A command centre had been set up in one of the Portakabins so he went in and explained who he was and where he was from. The St Anne's team was the first medical team to arrive on scene, and he didn't hesitate when the officer in charge asked him if they would work with the rescue crew that was digging out the survivors from the tunnel.

Owen went back to the group and explained what they were going to do. 'We'll split into two teams once we get inside the tunnel. Pete, you'll be working with me, and Rose will work with Rob.' He glanced at his registrar. 'Rose has experience of working at a major incident so let her guide you if you get stuck.'

'Will do!' Rob slung an arm around Rose's shoulders. 'Looks like it's you and me, kiddo. Rob and Rose—it has rather a nice ring to it, doesn't it? A bit like Batman and Robin.'

Owen turned away when everyone laughed. He certainly didn't intend to stand there worrying about the fact that his registrar seemed to be on very familiar terms with Rose. It wasn't his business what she did or who she did it with!

Picking up his hard hat, he led the way to the tunnel entrance where the rescue crew was waiting for them. It was a combined effort and the team was made up of members of the fire brigade's rescue service and engineers who'd been working on site. One of the firemen wrote down their names on the personnel list then introduced himself.

'I'm Chief Fire Officer Donald Grant and I'll be guiding you into the tunnel. We're just waiting for the all-clear before we head inside. The roof is still a bit unstable in places, so our guys are working with the engineers to shore it up.'

'How far along the tunnel were the men working when the roof caved in?' Owen asked.

'Just over a mile, so it will take a good ten minutes to reach them. We've brought the walking wounded out, but we didn't want to take any chances and move the rest until we got your say-so.'

He broke off when one of his men appeared from inside the tunnel. They conferred briefly before he turned to them again.

'We can go in now. Just take your time. There's a lot of rubble about in there. Oh, and if I tell you to get out, do so immediately. I don't want any dead heroes on my watch today.'

Owen shot an uneasy glance at Rose. He couldn't help wishing that she wasn't coming along on this trip. It was going to be dangerous work, from the sound of it, and he hated to think that she might be putting herself at risk.

His heart plummeted as he followed Donald Grant into the tunnel. He shouldn't have been thinking along those lines and couldn't understand why he was. However, there was no point trying to deny how he felt. The thought of Rose getting injured was a painful one, even though he wasn't prepared to examine the reasons behind it too closely.

Rose could feel the tension mounting as they made their way along the tunnel. It was an eerie feeling to know that they were walking beneath the streets of the capital. Although the tunnel was well lit, it was unnerving to know that they were deep underground. She was glad when Rob caught up with her.

'Creepy, isn't it? I travel on the tube every day, yet I never really think about the fact that I'm underground. This is different, though. There's no mistaking where you are when you can see all this.'

'There isn't,' she agreed with a shudder, glancing around at the walls of earth. Iron meshwork had been fixed around the sides and to the roof of the tunnel, but it looked very insubstantial to her inexperienced eyes. When they started to descend to a lower level she found herself wishing that she'd accepted Owen's offer and gone back to the hospital.

'Are you OK?'

She blinked when Rob tapped her on the shoulder. 'I think so.' She gave a little grimace. 'I'm supposed to be looking after you, not the other way round.'

'How about we look after each other?' Rob suggested, grinning at her. 'That's what superheroes do, isn't it? They watch each other's backs.'

'Sounds fair enough to me. You watch my back, Batman, and I'll watch yours!' she agreed with a laugh, feeling some of her tension ease.

'I must remember that line and use it again.' Rob chuckled. 'Most girls would freak out if I offered to watch them, but obviously it's different when you're in superhero mode!'

He leered suggestively at her. Rose shook her head. 'You are a complete idiot, do you know that?'

'Yes. But you love me anyway, don't you?' he declared, hamming it up for all he was worth as he stared at her with love-struck devotion.

Rose was just about to disabuse him of that idea but her pithy retort never got aired because Owen, who had been in front of them, suddenly turned round.

'It would help if you two kept your minds on the job. This isn't the school playground, in case you hadn't realised it.'

Rob looked suitably abashed as he dropped back a step, but Rose was incensed. How dared Owen speak to her like that in front of everyone? She was about to remonstrate with him when the chief fire officer held up his hand and signalled for them to stop.

'This is as far as we can go with any degree of ease. The next stretch is more difficult—you'll have to crawl in a couple of places. Don't worry, though. The roof has been made safe and it's just five or six yards before the tunnel widens out again. Single file, folks. I'll go first and one of my guys will bring up the rear to stop you escaping.'

A couple of people chuckled, but for the most part Rose could tell that everyone felt as nervous as she did. She followed Owen to the narrow section of the tunnel, glancing up in surprise when he suddenly turned round.

'It will be OK, Rose. Just take your time and you'll be fine.'

He didn't wait for her to reply, which was probably a good thing because she wouldn't have known what to say. The fact that he'd taken time to reassure her after admonishing her a few seconds earlier made her feel more mixed up than ever. He gave every appearance of disliking her, so why did he care if she was scared?

It was impossible to answer that question, yet as she followed him along the tunnel her heart felt a little bit lighter all of a sudden. Maybe Owen didn't dislike her quite as much as he tried to make out?

CHAPTER SIX

OWEN was relieved when the tunnel widened out again. It had been uncomfortable, crawling along the confined space, and even more so when he'd been so conscious that Rose was right behind him. He'd seen how nervous she looked, and he hated to imagine how scary she must have found it. He stood up abruptly, suddenly impatient with himself. There were more important issues to worry about than Rose's attack of the jitters.

Once everyone had made it safely through the narrow part of the tunnel, Donald Grant led them along the last lap. Arclights had been set up near where the roof had fallen in and they cast an eerie glow over the scene.

'We know there are five more men still trapped beneath the rubble,' Donald told them when they halted. 'We're not sure how long it's going to take to dig them out so it's going to be rather noisy in here. Just make sure that you listen out for my instructions in case I need you to evacuate the area.'

Owen nodded, deeming it wiser not to make too much of the instructions. There was no point making everyone more nervous than they already were. He pointed to where the injured men were lying. 'The sooner we get them checked over the faster we can move them out of here. Rose, can you start triage and sort out the most badly injured? We'll divide back into our teams once we know what we're dealing with.'

Rose hurried over to where the first of the injured was lying. Owen watched her kneel down beside the man, then turned away because she didn't need him standing guard over her. Rob followed him to where one man was lying a little apart from the others. He was unconscious and his breathing was very laboured. Owen knelt beside him and took a stethoscope out of his pack of medical supplies.

'No air entry on the left side,' he announced, listening to the man's chest. 'Right side entry is patchy, so we can't afford to waste any time.'

'Haemothorax?' Rob suggested, checking the man's pulse. 'Pulse is very fast. That's another indication of a haemothorax, isn't it?'

'It can be.' He examined the man's upper abdomen and nodded when he felt tension in the flesh. 'Yep, there's definitely something going on in there. With no access to X-rays we just have to trust our instincts, and our best bet is a haemothorax. It will need aspirating, so can I leave you to do that, Rob? You've done it before and you know the drill—just insert the needle between the ribs under his left arm and withdraw the blood that's collected in the pleural cavity.'

'Easy-peasy,' Rob agreed cheerfully, getting straight down to work.

Owen left him to it, pleased to see that the young registrar wasn't letting the strangeness of the situation get to him. It took a lot to put Rob down, he thought as he made his way to the next man. It was no wonder that Rose seemed to enjoy his company.

The thought was more distracting that it should have been, so he put it out of his mind as he knelt down. Two of the paramedics were attending to the man, so he checked that they were happy with his condition and moved on. Rose had worked her way down the line by then and she came hurrying over to him.

'There's three I'd like you to look at. The guy Pete is attending to and two others by the far wall. The man on the left has a GCS of eight.'

'I'll check him first.' He made his way over to where the workman was lying. He could see at a glance that the man had extensive head injuries and sighed. 'Doesn't look too promising, does it? Can you check his BP for me?'

Rose knelt down and quickly took a reading. He nodded when she told him what it was. 'Way too low. Let's get some fluid into him and send him off to hospital a.s.a.p. There's not much we can do for him here, I'm afraid.'

She took a cannula out of her pack and deftly inserted it into the back of the injured man's hand while Owen carried on with his examination. He shook his head when she looked questioningly at him.

'I can't find much sign of anything else, although something could show up on the X-rays. We'll put a collar on him and get him on a board, then ship him out.'

Rose selected a cervical collar and fitted it around the man's neck. The paramedics had brought a spinal board with them and they managed to slide the patient onto it without too much difficulty. Owen slipped an oxygen mask over the man's face, then cushioned head restraints were used to further protect him during the journey and he was strapped in. A shot of analgesic and they were ready to move him.

'We need to get him out of here as quickly as possible,' he explained, beckoning Donald over. The rescue crews were using a mechanical shovel to move some boulders and the noise was deafening—he had to shout to make himself heard above the din.

'I'll get a couple of my men to help,' the chief fire officer offered immediately. 'They'll need to manoeuvre him through that narrow section of the tunnel and it won't be easy.'

'Thanks. He's not going to survive if he doesn't get to hospital soon,' he explained. 'Even then, it's going to be touch and go. He's suffered a serious head trauma.'

'Are you sending one of your team with him?' Donald asked.

'No. The paramedics can cope from here on. They know what they're doing,' he replied, resisting the urge to ask Rose to accompany them. It was tempting to send her along and remove her from any possible danger, but she would be far more valuable to him here.

He left Donald to organise the move and went to check on the other casualties Rose had singled out. She was kneeling beside one of the men so he went straight over and examined him first.

'Fractured pelvis,' he said, listing the man's injuries as he found them. 'Right femur is fractured as well.' He slid his hand under the man's back. 'Definite misalignment in the lumbar spine, too.'

'I think he might have suffered a myocardial infarction as well. One of the other workmen told me that he'd been complaining of pains in his chest and jaw shortly before the roof caved in. They were about to call an ambulance when it happened.'

'It really isn't his day, is it?' he observed drolly, and Rose smiled.

'It certainly isn't. Do you want me to put in a line?'

'Please. I'm going to intubate him. We need to make sure that he doesn't move so I'll have to anaesthetise him.' Owen tried not to let her see how he was feeling. However, that smile had had an effect all right. Heat bubbles exploded in his veins and he abruptly stood up. 'I'll just check on the other guy first and come back to you.'

'Fine.'

She bent over the patient, blissfully unaware of what was happening and he was grateful for that. At least he had the comfort of knowing that she had no idea he was making a fool of himself. He went across to the other patient. Pete was with him and, unlike the previous casualties he'd seen, the young man Pete was attending to was conscious. He was obviously in pain, too, because he groaned when Owen crouched down beside him.

'Can you give me something for the pain, Doc? I'm in agony here.'

'Where does it hurt?'

'Just here.' He touched the left side of his chest, grimacing as another wave of pain hit him.

'You've probably cracked a couple of ribs.' Owen gently tested the area and nodded when he felt signs of crepitus—a grating sensation caused by the broken ends of bone rubbing together. 'Yes, just as I thought. It looks as though you've given yourself a really nasty knock.'

'Tell me about it.' The young man rolled his eyes. 'A chunk of rock hit me. Mind you, it could have been worse. If I hadn't managed to dive out of the way the whole roof would have landed on me and I'd have been squashed flat!'

'A lucky escape, from the sound of it. Anyway, I'll give you something for the pain.'

He told Pete what drugs he needed, then carried on with his examination while the nurse organised the shot. Although broken ribs could be extremely painful, they weren't normally a life-threatening injury so he was a little surprised that Rose had singled out this patient for urgent treatment.

'My name's Owen Gallagher, by the way,' he explained as he examined the young man's hips and pelvis. Maybe Rose had spotted something he hadn't, and he didn't intend to overlook something vital by rushing.

'Tim Lawrence,' the young man replied.

'Have you been working on the tunnel for very long?' he asked, discounting the pelvic area as a source of any major problems.

'It's my first week on the job. I only took it because I want to earn a bit of extra money before I go to university this autumn. I'm just back from a gap-year trip to Australia and I thought it would be a good way to boost my finances. Little did I know what I was letting myself in for.'

'Tough luck,' Owen observed sympathetically. He checked Tim's spine next, but found nothing there to alarm him so gave him the shot of morphine Pete had prepared for him, still unsure why Rose had decided the young man was in urgent need of treatment. There had to be a reason for her decision, because she was far too experienced a nurse to waste his time.

The thought that he trusted her clinical judgement was unsettling in view of their rocky relationship to date. However, he refused to let his personal feelings stand in the way of doing his job properly. He decided to re-examine Tim's chest, just to be on the safe side. His lung sounds were good, with air entry on both sides, so he could rule them out, and there was no problem with his heart. However, he frowned when he detected an unusual degree of swelling in the upper left part of the young man's abdomen.

'This is pretty swollen, even allowing for you having busted a couple of ribs.'

'All I know is that it hurts like mad,' Tim muttered.

'The shot will soon take the edge off it,' he assured him as he considered the implications of what he had found. A severe blow like that could have done more than simply fracture a couple of ribs. The spleen lay in this area of the abdomen and he couldn't rule out the possibility that it had been ruptured. If that was the case, Tim would need an emergency splenectomy to remove it otherwise he could bleed to death.

Owen came to a swift decision, knowing that he couldn't afford to take any chances. 'It's possible your spleen has been damaged, so I'm going to send you straight off to hospital.'

'My spleen?' Tim said, turning pale. 'Does that mean I'll need an operation?'

'It might well do. However, the good news is that your spleen isn't all that important once you're an adult. There'll be a slightly increased risk of you contracting infections if it's removed, but that's basically it.'

'Will I be out of action for very long?' Tim asked anxiously. 'I'm going to be really stuck if I can't work before I go to uni. I was relying on what I was going to earn to help pay for my accommodation.'

'If you do need the operation, you'll be in hospital for between six to ten days, then need a couple more weeks to recuperate. But you should be fine after that.' Owen clapped him on the shoulder. 'You'll be OK. Really you will.'

Tim didn't say anything as Owen asked Pete to start him on a drip. The young man was obviously shocked by what had happened to him. Once everything was done, Owen arranged for Tim to be moved immediately to hospital. Another team of medics had arrived by then, so that took the pressure off them a bit. As he went back to Rose he was feeling pretty confident about the outcome. Another half-hour and they should be on their way back to the hospital.

His gaze landed on Rose and he felt a sudden tightening in his chest. Once they were back at the hospital his problems wouldn't be over, though. There was still the matter of Daniel to worry about. Maybe he did trust her clinical judgement, but could he trust her with his son?

Rose wished that Owen would hurry up and come back. In the past couple of minutes the patient's condition had deteriorated and he was showing definite signs of slipping into VF. She looked up in relief when Owen appeared.

'He's not looking too good,' she explained, moving aside as he crouched down beside her. 'His heartbeat is very irregular. I think he's slipping into VF.'

'Let me take a look.'

His tone was cool as he bent over the man and she frowned. She had the distinct impression that he was upset, yet she had no idea what she'd done to annoy him. It was on the tip of her tongue to ask him what was wrong when it struck her how stupid it would be. Everything she did seemed to upset him!

'I'll give him a shot of lignocaine to settle things down, then intubate him. He's going to need bagging until we can get him on a ventilator, so can you get one of the paramedics over here to help?'

'Don't you want me to do it?' she said in surprise.

'No. You go and see if Rob needs any help. Pete can assist me once he's finished with his patient.'

'Fine.' Rose didn't argue as she stood up. She could tell there was no point. Maybe Owen had decided that enough was enough and working with her for any longer was too much.

The thought hurt, but she refused to dwell on it as she went over to the paramedics and relayed his instructions. Rob was dealing with a broken leg when she went to join him—he looked up and grinned at her.

'Just in time to help me fix this splint, Robin.'

Rose summoned a smile, refusing to let Owen's attitude get her down. 'You mean to say a superhero like you can't manage on your own?'

'Every superhero needs a sidekick to perform the menial tasks,' he told her, smirking.

'Hmm, I left myself wide open for that, didn't I?' She crouched down and helped him fit the inflatable splint to the man's left leg. It was difficult to fit it correctly without moving the limb and she sighed when the patient groaned. 'Sorry. I know it must hurt, but it will only take another few seconds now.'

'It's OK, love. I can put up with a bit of discomfort from you.' The elderly workman winked at her. 'It's been a long time since I had a lovely young woman ministering to me.'

Rose chuckled. 'Nice to know that I still fall into the *young* category. I've a birthday coming up next week and I'm starting to feel really old.'

'How old is old?' Rob put in, securing the Velcro strip that bound the top sections of the splint together.

'Old enough not to want to tell you,' she retorted.

'Oh, come on! You can't be *that* old.' Rob sat back on his heels and studied her thoughtfully. 'I'd say you're about twenty-eight or -nine—a year or so older than me.'

'Wrong!' Rose carefully eased the bottom section of the splint together and taped it in place.

'You mean you're older than that?' He shook his head. 'No way. You're having me on. I don't believe you're thirty.'

'And then some,' she replied with a laugh. She dusted off her hands and stood up. 'OK, so what's next?'

Rob explained to the man that he would be moved as soon as the paramedics came back and got up as well. 'That's about it until they dig out the others. And there's no knowing how long that will take or what state they're going to be in either.'

He drew her aside as the paramedics arrived to transport their patient above ground. The mechanical diggers had stopped working now, but there was still a lot of activity as the rescue team continued their efforts to reach the trapped men. He had to stand very close to her to make himself heard.

'Were you serious just now about your age? I can't believe you're that much older than me.'

'I'll be thirty-five next week,' she told him honestly. Although it was flattering to know that he thought she was the same age as him, there was no point lying. Not when she was going to meet her eighteen-year-old son at the weekend.

Instinctively, her gaze moved to Owen, and she felt a shiver skim down her spine when she realised he was watching them. Even though they weren't doing anything wrong, she was immediately on the defensive.

Stepping away from Rob, she made her way back to the

workman and checked that the paramedics were ready to move him. Everyone had been attended to by then and she wasn't surprised when Donald Grant told them they would be leaving very shortly. Now that the other crews had arrived on scene, they could deal with the rest of the casualties when they were dug out. It was back to base for the St Anne's team, and back to square one as far as she was concerned.

Had she really hoped that Owen's attitude might have softened while they'd been working together? She hated to think she was so naïve but she knew it was true. However, nothing had changed. He still didn't trust her, still didn't believe she should play any part in Daniel's life.

If she'd thought for a moment that meeting her would harm Daniel, she wouldn't have agreed to see him. However, from the impression she'd formed when they'd spoken on the phone, this meeting was as important to Daniel as it was to her. Now nothing was going to stand in the way of doing what was right for her son, and if that meant going against Owen's wishes, that was what she would do. It was just a shame that they seemed to be on opposite sides when they wanted the same thing. They both wanted Daniel to be happy.

CHAPTER SEVEN

ROSE managed to hitch a ride back to the hospital with the same crew who had ferried her to the tunnel. She spent the journey talking to the elderly workman who'd suffered the leg injuries. His name was Alan Bradbury and he told her that he was due to retire later that year. He regaled her with tales of his experiences of working on various engineering projects, so that before she knew it they'd reached the hospital.

'I'll check on you later,' Rose told him as the crew opened the rear doors. 'I expect you'll be going up to Orthopaedics once your leg has been sorted out, so I'll pop in to see you before I go off duty.'

'You do that, love. It will do my image the power of good to have a beautiful young woman asking after me,' he told her cheerily.

Rose laughed as she jumped down from the ambulance and hurried inside. It was nice to be appreciated for once! Charlie was crossing the waiting area when she arrived and he stopped to speak to her.

'Made it back safely, I see. So how did it go?'

'Not too badly, all things considered. What about the patients we sent back here—in particular, the guy with the head injury and the man who had a suspected spinal injury?'

'The head injury is in Theatre—I'm not sure what the outcome will be. As for the other guy, I'm afraid he didn't make it. He suffered a massive myocardial infarction on his way here and the paramedics weren't able to resuscitate him.'

'What a shame. How about the young man with the broken ribs? I had a feeling there was more to it than that...' She shrugged, unable to explain the feeling she'd had. Had it been the fact that the patient was close to Daniel's age which had made her ultra-careful? she wondered.

'You were right, too. He had a ruptured spleen. If he hadn't been brought in PDQ he might not have made it either, but he's out of Theatre now and he's going to be fine. Anyway, leave your coveralls in the bin in the storeroom—they'll need cleaning—then you can take a break.'

'Are you sure?' she queried, glancing at the rows of people who were waiting to be seen. The automated display board above the reception desk was giving a waiting time of four hours—their absolute maximum under current government guidelines.

'Yes. You need to wind down after an operation like that. Isn't that right, Owen?'

'Isn't what right?'

Rose swung round when she heard Owen's voice. He must have arrived shortly after she had got there, because he was standing right behind her. She couldn't help noticing how tired and strained he looked, and her heart immediately went out to him.

'Charlie was insisting that I should take a break. Maybe you should take one, too. You look all in.'

'I suggest you leave me to decide whether I'm fit to do my job,' he said brusquely, striding past her.

Rose felt the embarrassed colour sweep up her cheeks and hurried away. However, she knew that Charlie must be wondering why Owen had spoken to her in that fashion. He'd been little short of rude, and there had been no call for it when she'd been trying to help.

She sighed as she made her way to the storeroom. That was the whole point, though; Owen didn't want her help. He didn't want anything to do with her. She was a nuisance, someone who threatened his relationship with Daniel, and if he could find a way to erase her from their lives, he would do so. She couldn't understand why she kept hoping the situation would improve when there was no likelihood of it happening. Owen had set out to dislike her and he wasn't about to change his mind.

By the time she'd stowed away her protective clothing Rose was feeling uncharacteristically gloomy. She decided that she would do as Charlie had suggested and take a break, in the hope it would lift her spirits. The canteen was on the fifth floor, so she made her way up there and bought a cup of a coffee and a sandwich. It was lunchtime and the place was packed; she was looking for somewhere to sit when Rob arrived.

'Hang on a sec and I'll find us a table,' he told her, grabbing a tray. He loaded a double portion of lasagne onto it, added a large cup of coffee then went to the till.

'How about the balcony?' he suggested, after he'd paid. 'It's just about warm enough to sit outside today. I don't know about you, but I could do with a bit of fresh air after being stuck down that giant rat hole all morning.'

'Sounds good to me,' she agreed, chuckling at his rather apt description of the multi-billion-pound extension to the tube. She followed him out to the balcony, breathing in deeply as she put her tray on the table. 'I must say, the air does smell remarkably good up here. It's hard to believe we're in the middle of London.'

'The worst of the fumes tend to hang around at ground level, thankfully enough,' Rob explained, unloading his lunch. 'If I were in charge of the city then I'd be thinking about building skyways rather than walkways.'

'A novel idea.' Rose pulled out a chair and sat down. 'Maybe you should suggest it to the powers that be.'

'I doubt they'd take much notice of a humble registrar,' Rob said wryly, forking up a huge mouthful of pasta.

'You never know until you try,' she retorted.

'Hmm. Maybe not, although I'm not sure I have the energy to go into politics as well as medicine. It takes me all my time to keep Owen happy, and I don't think he'd be too pleased if I tried to diversify.'

'Has he always been so exacting?' she asked, peeling the plastic film off her sandwich.

'He's always been very focused, from what I've seen. However, most people who've worked with him for a while— like Angie, for instance—say that he's become far more demanding since his wife died. She had cancer,' he added as an afterthought.

'I see.'

Rose deemed it wiser not to mention that she already knew about Owen's wife in case it gave rise to any awkward questions. She bit into her sandwich, but the urge to find out more about him was too tempting to resist. 'Do you think he's become more demanding because he feels that he let his wife down?'

'What do you mean?' Rob said in surprise. 'From what I know, she had the very best care available, so why should Owen feel responsible for her death?'

'I can't speak from experience, but I know several people who've felt guilty because they weren't able to do more to help their loved ones.' She shrugged. 'It's understandable when you think about it. Here you are with all this medical knowledge at your fingertips, yet you can't do anything to help the people you love most of all.'

'I never thought about it that way,' Rob said thoughtfully.

'It might apply, though, don't you think? Owen blames himself because he wasn't able to save his wife. That's why it's so important for him to do all he can for his patients.'

* * *

Owen ground to a halt when he heard what Rose had said. He'd decided to eat his lunch on the terrace because it would be quieter out there. He knew that he'd been far too sharp with her when he'd got back to the hospital but he'd had his reasons.

He'd bumped into Mike Gerard, his opposite number from the Royal, as he had been leaving the tunnel, and in the course of their conversation Mike had mentioned that he knew Rose. Apparently she had worked at the Royal before she had started to do agency work.

It had been too good an opportunity to miss; Owen hadn't been able to resist finding out more about her. Although Mike had been highly complimentary about her nursing skills, he had been less enthusiastic about her personally. After a little careful probing, Owen had discovered that she had gained a reputation for walking away after she had ditched one of his friend's colleagues. According to Mike, she had a problem when it came to commitment and it had been the last thing he'd wanted to hear when he was already so concerned about her letting Daniel down.

Now he wasn't sure what angered him most—the fact that she of all people had had the temerity to criticise his behaviour, or that her assessment had been so accurate. He *did* blame himself for not being able to do more for Laura, and it stung to know how accurately Rose had summed him up.

'When I need psychoanalysing, I shall get professional help,' he said, his voice grating with anger. He saw the shock on her face when she swung round, but it was of little consolation. 'In the meantime, I would appreciate it if you kept your opinions to yourself, Ms Tremayne. My private life is not open for discussion.'

He spun round on his heel, forgetting that he'd been about to sit down and eat his lunch. It was only when he reached the door and realised he had the tray in his hands that he remembered. Stacking the tray in the rack, he strode out of the canteen, wondering if he had ever felt so angry before. The thought of Rose sitting there, talking about him like that, was more than he could stand.

'Wait!'

He didn't pause when he heard her calling to him, didn't even glance round. He'd seen and heard more than enough for one day and the best thing she could do now was to leave him alone.

'I'm sorry, Owen. Really I am.'

The plea in her voice made him hesitate and she took advantage of the fact. She ran the last couple of yards and stopped in front of him. Owen felt a little pang of regret shoot through him when he saw the anguish on her face, but he snuffed it out. She wasn't going to get round him that easily!

'I never meant to upset you. Rob and I were just chatting—'

'About me.' He laughed shortly. 'Yes, I heard what you said.'

'I know, and I'm sorry because I never meant to…well, hurt you.' She laid her hand on his arm and he stiffened when he felt her fingers gripping his flesh. It was all he could do not to snatch his arm away, but that would have been far too revealing.

'I am not upset,' he said, coldly enunciating every word. 'I'm angry because you seem to think that you have the right to meddle in my affairs.'

'I don't! Why won't you ever listen to what I'm saying? Why do you always think the worst of me?'

'Because you've given me no reason to think anything good.'

He shrugged off her hand, past caring how she might interpret the action. It didn't matter what she thought; it only mattered that he removed her hand before it caused any more damage. Even now he could feel ripples of sensation spreading from the point where her fingers had rested, hot little flurries that were filtering into his body like miniature earthquakes. He could feel the shock waves rolling outwards and downwards until his whole being seemed to be suffused with sensation and it was the last thing he needed, the final straw. He didn't want her anywhere near him!

He brushed past her and went to the lift, praying that she would have the sense not to follow him. For two long years he'd held himself together, yet all of a sudden it seemed as though everything was caving in on him. He should have done more to help Laura! He should have tried harder to persuade her to tell Daniel the truth! He should have seen how devastated his son had been and done more to help him, too! He had failed both Laura and Daniel, so what kind of a man must he be when he couldn't protect the two people he loved most in the whole world?

Pain washed through him as he stepped into the lift, but he deserved it and more. He stabbed his finger on a button and waited for the doors to close, wishing that he could close his mind to this agony he felt. Oh, he'd done a good job of pretending that he was fine in the past couple of years—most people had believed him, too. But he hadn't been able to hide the truth from Rose, had he…?

'Please! You must listen to me.'

Owen flinched when Rose slid into the lift before the doors closed. He pressed the stop button but it was too late—they were already moving. He glared at her. 'I don't know what you hope to achieve by this—'

'I just want to say I'm sorry! For heaven's sake, Owen, I'm not some kind of monster.' She glared back at him, her blue eyes staring directly into his. He could see the anger they held but it was mixed with regret, and maybe it was that which made him do what he did next.

Reaching out, he hauled her into his arms and kissed her. It was the briefest, fiercest kiss imaginable, yet none the less potent because of that. He groaned when his senses suddenly ran wild. All he could think about was how soft her lips were, how sweet her breath tasted, how silky smooth her skin felt. And when she gave a tiny helpless murmur and kissed him back he was completely overwhelmed.

The lift stopped with a jolt that brought him back to his senses. He just had time to push her away before the doors sprang open. Rose swung round and walked out of the lift without a word, and he followed her because there was nothing else he could do. He couldn't stay in there, hiding away from what he'd done, couldn't pretend it hadn't happened, couldn't even blame her. He was responsible for his own actions. He had kissed her because he had wanted to. And his punishment was to be left wondering why she had kissed him back.

Rose had no idea how she got through the rest of the day. She seemed to be on autopilot, doing what was asked of her without conscious thought. What had happened in the lift had turned her world upside down. The fact that Owen had kissed her had been shocking enough, but it was the fact that she'd kissed him back which really scared her.

He'd made no secret of his dislike for her, yet she couldn't deny that she was attracted to him. It made her see how dangerous the situation was becoming. She couldn't afford to make any mistakes when they could have an impact on her relationship with Daniel.

She signed her worksheet then went to fetch her coat, wondering if she should contact the agency and ask them to find a replacement for her. Working at St Anne's was going to be very stressful after what had happened and she wasn't sure if she was up to dealing with the repercussions.

It would be easier if she left, yet she was loath to let Owen think she was leaving because of what had happened. They were bound to meet again if she saw Daniel on a regular basis, and she hated to imagine how awkward it would be with the memory of that kiss hanging over them. Maybe it would be better if she tried to forget about it. It shouldn't be too hard because she doubted if Owen would mention it again. The easiest solution might be to blot it out of her mind…if she could.

Saturday dawned, clear and bright. Rose was up before seven and showered and dressed before she went into the kitchen to make herself some breakfast. She made a pot of tea and some toast but her appetite seemed to have deserted her. She kept thinking about what was going to happen when she met Daniel. Would she recognise him?

She'd never thought to ask him to send her a photograph of himself and couldn't bear to think that she might not know who he was. Maybe she should have arranged to carry something to make the process easier—a rolled-up newspaper or an umbrella—anything at all that would have singled her out from the crowd. She was on the verge of telephoning him to suggest it when it struck her that Owen might answer, and she really didn't want to speak to him when she was already so nervous.

By the time she left her flat she'd worked herself up into such a state that she could barely think straight. Fortunately, the bus was on time for once and it didn't take very long to get to Hyde Park. Rose made her way straight to the Serpentine. There were a lot of people in the park, and she had to weave her way through all the skaters and joggers, but she finally reached the café where she'd arranged to meet Daniel.

She was ten minutes early, so she found a bench and sat down, hoping she would spot him amongst the crowd. Owen had never said anything about what the boy looked like, so she had no idea if Daniel resembled her. He'd had blond hair when he was born and blue eyes, too, but that could have changed…

Her breath caught when she saw him walking towards her. There wasn't a doubt in her mind about who he was as she rose unsteadily to her feet. His hair was the same honey-gold colour as hers was, and as he came closer she could see that his eyes were exactly the same shade of blue.

When he stopped in front of her, she saw myriad expressions cross his face, and knew he could see the same expressions on hers. This was her child, her son, the baby she had given away eighteen years ago, and for a second she wasn't sure what to do—before instinct took over.

Stepping forward, Rose put her arms around him and hugged him, held him tightly against her heart as she'd longed to do so many times over the years. No matter what happened from this point on she would have this moment to cherish: her son was back in her arms, where he should always have been.

CHAPTER EIGHT

OWEN felt a lump come to his throat as he watched Rose hugging his son. He couldn't remember seeing such a wealth of emotion on anyone's face before. He had tried not to think about how she might feel when she met Daniel, but it was impossible to ignore how much this meeting meant to her. Just for a second he tried to imagine how he would feel if he were in her place—meeting his child for the first time in years—but it was too painful.

He turned away, suddenly feeling as though he was intruding on a private moment that had nothing to do with him. It had been Daniel's idea that he should come along. The boy had been very nervous at the thought of meeting Rose and had begged him to go with him, otherwise he wouldn't have been there. However, he doubted if Daniel or Rose needed him now, and the thought filled him with an overpowering sense of loneliness.

'Dad, wait!'

Owen stopped when he heard Daniel shouting to him. He turned around, seeing the surprise on Rose's face. Obviously it had never occurred to her that he might turn up for this meeting, and he could tell that she wasn't thrilled to see him. He couldn't blame her, of course—not after what had happened in the lift the other day.

Heat flowed through him and he had to make a conscious

effort not to betray his feelings as Daniel came hurrying over to him. He'd tried his best to forget about that kiss, but far too many times he'd found himself remembering how sweet her lips had tasted. He might not trust Rose, but he had enjoyed kissing her and there was no point pretending otherwise. It made it doubly difficult to appear in control of himself when Daniel reached him.

'Don't you want to meet Rose?' the boy asked, obviously puzzled by his apparent lack of interest.

'I didn't want to intrude,' he explained, wondering if he should have told Daniel that he'd already met her. It had seemed too complicated at first, but he would hate Daniel to think he'd been withholding information, especially when he had no idea what Rose might say.

'Of course you're not intruding!' Daniel declared fiercely. 'Look, at least come and say hello. Then Rose and I can go and have a chat, and meet up with you later.'

'If you're sure?'

Owen did his best to disguise his lack of enthusiasm but there was little he could do apart from refuse to meet her, and that would have complicated matters even more. He followed Daniel back to where Rose was waiting, trying not to notice how pretty she looked that day. Jeans and a soft lemon-yellow sweater made the most of her slender figure, emphasising the length of her legs and the neat curve of her waist. She'd tied her blonde hair back into a ponytail and she looked far too young to be the mother of an eighteen-year-old son.

'Rose, this is my dad: Owen Gallagher.'

'We've already met.' Rose smiled coolly as she held out her hand. 'I'm a nurse, you see, and I've been working at St Anne's for the past week.'

'Really? Wow!' Daniel turned to him in delight. 'I can't believe that you two know each other. How cool is that?'

'It's a small world,' Owen replied evenly, taking her outstretched hand. Her fingers curled around his for a second before she withdrew them, but it was long enough to set off a whole chain of reactions.

Owen let his hand fall to his side. His palm felt hot, as though his skin had been scorched by the fleeting contact with hers. Even his fingertips felt warm and kind of tingly. He ran his hand down the seam of his trousers but the sensations didn't go away. It was as though just by touching him Rose had left her mark on him for ever.

The thought alarmed him, because there was no way that he wanted to feel this way. He turned to Daniel, hoping his son couldn't tell how on edge he was feeling. 'I'm going to make myself scarce now. How about we meet up back here at one o'clock—would that be OK?'

'I should think so.' Daniel looked uncertainly at Rose. 'You don't have to spend that much time with me if you don't want to, of course. You might have things to do…'

'There's nothing I want more than to spend some time with you, Daniel,' she said softly.

'Great!' Daniel's face broke into a wide smile. 'It will give us a chance to get to know one another.'

'I'll see you later, then.' Owen turned away because he couldn't bear to see him looking so excited. Daniel was so very vulnerable and he was terrified that he would get hurt.

He made his way back along the path, wondering how he was going to fill in the time until he could go back and meet him. Just the thought of what might happen in the interim almost tore him in two, but he had to hope that Rose had meant what she'd said about not doing anything to hurt their son.

His breath caught as the full weight of the phrase *their son* struck him. Daniel wasn't just his son now, he was Rose's son, as well, now that she'd met him. There was no point pretending that it didn't alter the dynamics of their relationship. He would have to learn to share Daniel and he wasn't sure if he could do that. Daniel was the most important person in his life, and he couldn't help worrying how it was going to affect his relationship with him if he had to add Rose to the equation.

He also couldn't help worrying about the effect it was going to have in other areas of his life as well. There was no point pretending that he didn't find her attractive—that episode in the lift had disproved that once and for all! But it would be wrong to allow the attraction to develop. The situation was complicated enough without that!

The two hours Rose spent with Daniel flew past. They found a quiet spot beneath some trees where they could sit down on the grass and talk.

Daniel asked her a lot of questions, and listened attentively while she described her childhood growing up as an only child in a small Cornish village. He seemed interested in everything she had to say, but Rose guessed that he was leading up to the main question he wanted to ask her, which was why she'd had him adopted. She had already decided that she was going to tell him the truth. Even though she had no idea how he would react, it was important that he knew all the facts. It would be up to him what happened after that.

'Did you never think of keeping me when you found out you were pregnant?' he said diffidently when she paused.

'Yes, I did. I made up my mind that I was going to bring you up myself. Only things didn't work out the way I hoped they would.'

She glanced down, steeling herself before she continued, because she still found it hard to talk about that period in her life. 'My parents were horrified when they found out I was pregnant. They tried to persuade me to have an abortion, and when I refused they sent me to stay with a distant cousin who lived just outside London. They didn't want everyone in the village finding out, you see.'

'It must have been really hard, having to go and live with strangers,' Daniel said quietly.

'It was. I didn't know a soul in the area, and the people I was staying with weren't exactly sympathetic to my plight. I think they'd only agreed to take me in because my parents had paid them.'

'How old were you?'

'Just seventeen.' She shrugged. 'At least I was someplace safe and not living on the streets, which is what happens to a lot of young girls.'

'I suppose so. So what happened after I was born? Did you go back home then?'

'No, I never went home again. I had hoped that my parents would accept the idea of me having a baby once you were born, but they didn't. When I phoned them and told them that I intended to keep you they refused to have anything more to do with me. The people I'd been staying with had made it clear that I couldn't return to their house, so I had to find somewhere else to live when I came out of hospital.

'I came to London and stayed in a hostel while I found us a place to live. I was determined that I would manage somehow, but I soon realised how impossible it was going to be to provide for you. I was just seventeen years old and I had no qualifications and little hope of getting a decent job. Added to that, the flat I'd found for us was in a very rough area—we were burgled three times in the first month we were living there and all our belongings were either trashed or stolen. There was also a lot of violence and drugtaking on the estate, and it was that which convinced me in the end that I had to let you be adopted. I couldn't bear to imagine what might happen if we had to live there while you were growing up.'

'I see.' He bit his lip, and Rose could tell that he was upset by what he'd heard.

'I wish I could have kept you, Daniel. It broke my heart to

have to part with you, but I did it because I loved you. I wanted you to have all the things I couldn't provide for you. I wanted you to have a happy and secure life.'

'What about my father? Couldn't he have helped? Or didn't he know about me?'

Rose sighed when she heard the belligerence in his voice. 'Yes, he knew about you, but he didn't want to get involved. He'd just finished his finals and a baby wasn't part of his plans for the future.'

'So he just *dumped* you when he found out you were pregnant?'

'Yes. I suppose you could put it that way.'

'And you've never heard from him since?' he persisted.

'No. I can tell you his name, if you want to know it, but I have no idea where he's living now. I haven't seen him since before you were born.'

'There doesn't seem much point if he's not interested,' he said bitterly.

'Don't think too badly of him, Daniel. He just wasn't ready for fatherhood and couldn't cope with the responsibility of having a child.'

'Maybe not, but he could have done something. You wouldn't have had to give me away if somebody had helped you!'

'No, probably I wouldn't. But people do what they think is right at the time,' she explained gently. 'I did what I thought was right for you, and it seems to have worked out pretty well, doesn't it?'

'Yeah, I suppose. I had a happy childhood. Mum and Dad were great parents—they did everything they could for me.' He bit his lip and she could see the glitter of tears in his eyes. 'Mum died of cancer two years ago. It was awful, it really cut me up to lose her, especially as I had no idea what was happening. Mum and Dad didn't tell me what was going on, you see.'

'Maybe they wanted to spare you a lot of heartache,' she said quietly, remembering what Owen had told her.

'Well, it didn't! I knew Mum was ill, of course. It was obvious. But I didn't know *how* ill she was. I didn't know she was going to die!' He ran his hands over his face, obviously embarrassed about showing his feelings in front of her.

'I expect they thought it was the best thing to do at the time.'

'Then they were wrong! If they'd told me what was happening, it wouldn't have been such a shock when Mum died. I did some really stupid things after that, like drinking too much and smoking pot. I just went completely off the rails.'

'Grief affects people in different ways. You mustn't blame yourself because you weren't thinking clearly.'

'I thought you'd be horrified when I told you that,' he said in astonishment.

'Obviously I would hate to think you hadn't learned your lesson from it, but we all do things we're ashamed of, Daniel. The secret is to not repeat our mistakes.'

'I wish Dad felt like that. He seems to think I'm going to mess up again if he doesn't watch me like a hawk. He treats me like a five-year-old most of the time—always on my case about getting my college work done.'

Rose laughed at the disgust in his voice. 'I'm afraid that's par for the course when you're a teenager. Parents always think they know best. But you have to remember that your father only nags you because he loves you and wants what is best for you.'

'I know he does. And I know that Mum's death hit him really hard, too.' He sighed. 'I just wish he'd try to get on with his life—go out and have some fun for a change. It's what Mum would have wanted him to do.'

'It takes time to get over losing someone you love,' she said quietly, her heart aching at the thought of what Owen was still suffering. He must have loved his wife very much, and the thought sent a little pang of regret coursing through her.

'And, talking about your father, isn't it time you went to meet him?' she added, blanking out the thought. It was pointless worrying about it. Owen certainly wouldn't thank her for her concern—he'd probably accuse her of poking her nose in where it wasn't wanted!

'Is that really the time?' Daniel leapt to his feet, looking ill at ease all of a sudden. 'I've really enjoyed meeting you today, Rose. I'd like to see you again, if that's OK with you?'

'I'd love to see you again, too. I can't begin to tell you how much today has meant to me. I won't even try in case I embarrass you!' She smiled when he laughed, although she could tell he was pleased to hear her say that. 'Maybe you could give me a call when you've got some free time? I don't want to take you away from your studies, so I'll fit in with you. I don't work weekends at the moment, so I'm always free then.'

'That would be great!' He shuffled his feet, then suddenly stuck out his hand. 'Thanks, Rose. I know it wasn't easy for you to tell me about your parents and everything, but I'm glad you were honest with me.'

'Thank you for being so understanding,' she said, her voice thick with emotion. She shook his hand. 'I'll see you very soon, I hope.'

'Definitely.'

He gave her a grin, then loped off across the park. Rose watched until he was swallowed up by the crowd, then made her way to the gate. The meeting had gone far better than she'd dared hope it would, and now all she could do was wait for Daniel to get in touch with her. She wanted so much to see him again. Now that he was back in her life she didn't intend to lose him a second time, although it might not be up to her what happened, of course. Owen still wasn't happy about her seeing Daniel, and she doubted if he would try to foster a closer relationship between them.

She squared her shoulders. Maybe Owen wasn't keen on her seeing Daniel, but she wasn't going to let him get in the way of doing what she knew was right. Daniel needed her. And she was going to be there for him every step of the way!

* * *

Monday arrived and Owen was glad to go back to work. Daniel hadn't stopped talking about Rose all weekend. He had told Owen at length about Rose's parents refusing to help her and how his father had dumped her when he'd found out she was pregnant. Owen had made all the appropriate replies, but he really and truly hadn't wanted to hear all the details. He couldn't afford to start feeling sorry for her.

At least work acted as a distraction. The day got off to a brisk start when an RTA was brought in. Two women had been injured when they had swerved to avoid a dog which had run into the road. The driver, Marion Bates, was the most seriously injured, so he took charge of her and asked Suzanne to look after the passenger. Devinder Sharma—their new house officer—was on duty that morning, so Owen told him that he would like him to assist. It would be good experience for the younger doctor.

'I'm Owen Gallagher, consultant in charge of the trauma unit,' he explained as soon as the staff had transferred the woman onto a bed. 'And this is Dr Sharma, one of our house officers,' he added, nodding to Devinder, who was looking extremely nervous about his first stint in Resus. 'We're just going to examine you, so try to relax.'

'Can you get a message to my husband?' Marion moved the oxygen mask away from her face. 'I was only popping out to the shops to buy some milk, and he'll be wondering where I've got to.'

'Don't worry about that now. One of the nurses will sort it out for you.'

He glanced over his shoulder, feeling his heart lurch when he realised that Rose had now come into Resus. She hadn't been around when he'd arrived, and he couldn't pretend that the sight of her didn't affect him. He avoided looking at her as he summoned Julie over. 'Can you contact this lady's husband and let him know what's happened to her? The police should be able to give you the details.'

He returned his attention to the patient as the nurse hurried away. A quick check of the monitoring equipment assured him that Marion's heart-rate and BP were normal, and that her oxygen saturation levels were within acceptable limits. She'd had a GCS of ten when the paramedics had arrived on scene, and his main concern was a possible head injury.

'Did you lose consciousness when you crashed?' he asked, checking the rather large gash on her temple.

'I'm not sure. It's all a bit hazy, you see. One minute I was driving along the road and the next thing I knew there was this dog right in front of me. I swerved to avoid it and ran straight into a lamppost.'

'The paramedics said that the lamppost toppled onto your car.' He took the torch off the wall and used it to check how her pupils reacted to the light. The left one responded a shade more sluggishly than the right and he glanced at Devinder. 'Check Mrs Bates's response to light, will you, Dr Sharma?'

He moved aside to give the young doctor some room, uncoiling his stethoscope so he could listen to the woman's chest. There were sounds of air entry on both sides, so her breathing did not appear to have been compromised.

'Both pupils dilated evenly, sir.'

He glanced up when Devinder reported his findings. 'Check again, and pay particular attention to the left pupil,' he instructed, curbing his first instinct, which was to snap at the younger man. It took time to build up the skills needed to examine a patient properly, and he mustn't be impatient because the junior doctor hadn't spotted the problem. It wasn't Dr Sharma's fault that he was so on edge.

The thought made him grit his teeth. He knew the reason for his tension was having to work in such close proximity to Rose. Daniel's response to meeting her had been everything he'd feared it would be and it had reinforced all his doubts. However, it wasn't just his concern for Daniel that was making him so uneasy—it was the way *he* responded to her as well.

His gaze skimmed across the room and he felt a little spurt of awareness shoot through him as he saw her bend over the other patient. Her face was set with concentration, yet he knew that she was just as aware of him as he was of her. She suddenly looked round and he turned away, not wanting her to know that he had been watching her. Devinder had spotted the problem now, and Owen nodded when the younger doctor reported his findings, knowing that he couldn't afford to let his mind wander again.

'Good. It's not always easy to spot these things but you'll get better with practice. Mrs Bates will need a CT scan, so can you sort it out? Tell the radiologist that it's a priority case.'

He carried on with his examination but could find no other signs of any serious injuries. He asked Beth Humphreys to do the usual X-rays, then went to check how Suzanne was faring, steeling himself when Rose accidentally brushed against him as she reached up to replace the drip.

'Excuse me,' she murmured, stepping around him.

Owen didn't reply, not trusting himself to speak in case the tone of his voice gave him away. However, it was hard to ignore the frissons that were rippling through his body. Just the lightest touch seemed to set off a whole chain of reactions, and it worried him that he was so responsive to her. Was it the fact that he'd been celibate for such a long time that was making him react this way?

His sex life had been the least of his worries when Laura had been so ill. After she'd died he hadn't been interested in having a relationship with another woman. For two years he'd been celibate out of choice, yet all of a sudden his body was making its demands known. And it was the fact that it was Rose who had reawoken his desire that shocked him so much; Rose, who was the biggest threat to his peace of mind; Rose, the mother of his son. How could he possibly feel this way about her?

CHAPTER NINE

ROSE wasn't sure what was going through Owen's mind but she could tell there was something wrong, and it didn't take a genius to work out that it had to do with her.

She finished hanging a fresh bag of saline on the stand, wondering how soon she could make her escape. They were short-staffed that day, which was why Angie had asked her to work in Resus, but she would have preferred to put a bit more space between her and Owen…

He suddenly moved around the bed and she flinched when she found him standing in front of her. Colour swept up her face as she stepped aside, ignoring the speculative look Angie gave her. Picking up the soiled dressings, she took them to the clinical waste sack. Suzanne was updating Owen on the patient's progress so she decided to keep out of the way until they'd finished. There was no point courting trouble if she could avoid it.

The warning beep of a monitor suddenly rang around the room and she spun round. Devinder appeared to be rooted to the spot with shock as he stared at Marion Bates, who had arrested. Rose ran over to the bed and pushed him aside.

'I'll start CPR. Drop the head of the bed—she needs to be lying flat.'

The young doctor looked blankly at her, then suddenly came to his senses. He hurriedly lowered the head of the bed while she began chest compressions. Owen had arrived by then, and he nodded when he saw what she was doing.

'You carry on. Devinder, you sort out her breathing. I'll give her a shot of adrenaline and see if we can get her heart going again.'

One of the other nurses ran to fetch the drugs but Rose ignored what was happening around her as she carried on with the compressions.

'Pulse check,' Owen ordered, and she stopped while he checked the carotid artery in Marion's neck. He shook his head. 'Nothing yet.'

Rose took up her position again, concentrating all her energy on performing the lifesaving technique. Owen gave the patient a second shot of adrenaline then decided to defibrillate her when that didn't work either.

'Clear!' he ordered.

Everyone stepped back as he applied the paddles to Marion's chest and sent an electric current through her heart. The monitor suddenly beeped as sinus rhythm was established again and a collective sigh went up.

'I just froze when the monitor went off.' Devinder looked shaken as he slipped an oxygen mask over the woman's face. 'I forgot everything I know about resuscitating a patient who's arrested.'

'It's quite normal,' Rose said sympathetically.

'Maybe, but you didn't freeze, did you?' he pointed out.

'That's because I've done this loads of times before,' she assured him. 'The first time it happens to you is always the scariest.'

'I hope you're right.'

He didn't seem convinced, but Rose didn't say anything else. It wasn't up to her to deal with the junior medical staff's worries. She went back to her own patient and assisted Suzanne until the woman was ready to be transferred to a ward. Marion had been sent for a CT scan, so Rose helped to clear everything away then went back to the cubicles. She was just about to fetch her next patient when Owen appeared.

'Thanks for stepping in so smartly. I appreciate your help.'

Rose looked at him in surprise. It was the first time he'd said anything positive to her since she'd started working in his department. 'It's what I'm paid to do.'

'I know. I just wanted to thank you. That's all.'

His tone was brusque now, and she realised how ungracious she must have sounded. 'I'm sorry. I was just surprised that you said anything.'

'Meaning that I don't go handing out compliments very often?' he replied somewhat wryly.

'Well, it did seem a little out of character…'

'I bet it did.' He suddenly chuckled, his whole face lighting up. 'You don't need to worry about being tactful. I know my reputation for being a slave-driver!'

She laughed at that, delighted by the change in him. He looked so much more approachable when he laughed. 'I wouldn't go quite *that* far.'

'No? Then you must see me in a different light to everyone else.'

It was the kind of throw-away remark that people made all the time, yet Rose knew that she couldn't let it pass even though it might be a mistake to respond to it. Did she really want him to know how confused she felt—knowing he mistrusted her yet still attracted to him?

'I find it hard to separate your public persona from your private one—the loving father who does everything in his power to protect his son.' She shrugged, hoping that she hadn't said too much, but she felt too strongly about the issue to hide behind the accepted social mores. 'So, yes, maybe I do see you in a different light to everyone else, Owen.'

An expression of surprise crossed his face, but before he could reply, Suzanne appeared with a query she needed him to answer. Rose excused herself and hurried away. There were patients needing her attention so there was no excuse for wasting time. However, as she escorted her next patient into a cubicle, she realised that she would love to have the opportunity to get to know Owen better, and not just for Daniel's sake either. Now that she'd glimpsed the real man behind the forbidding exterior, she wanted to learn more about him.

Owen thought about the conversation he'd had with Rose on and off for the rest of the day. The fact that she seemed willing to forgive the way he'd behaved towards her had affected him deeply. He was also surprised that she'd dared to tell him the truth, although maybe he shouldn't have been after what Daniel had told him.

She had told Daniel the truth about the circumstances surrounding his birth, and not tried to put a gloss on the facts, as many other women might have done. He realised all of a sudden that he admired her honesty, and it was strange to feel such a positive emotion for a change. By the time Owen left work he knew that he needed to sort out his feelings with regard to Rose. Daniel was spending the night with one of his friends, which meant he didn't have to rush home, so he decided to treat himself to dinner and a film afterwards. It had been ages since he'd had a night out, and it might help to restore some balance to his life.

He had dinner at a restaurant near the hospital, then went to the early showing of the latest blockbuster movie. It was just gone nine when he left the cinema, and he still didn't feel like going home. He collected his car and drove across the city, but it was only when he found himself outside the block of flats where Rose lived that he finally admitted there had been nothing aimless about his journey. Everything he'd done that night had been leading up to this point: he wanted to see Rose and find out why she made him feel so confused.

* * *

Rose had just poured herself a glass of wine when the doorbell rang. She put the glass on the table and went to see who it was. She rarely had visitors in an evening, because most of her friends worked the same kind of unsocial hours she sometimes did. Pressing the speaker button, she asked who it was, and was stunned when she heard Owen's voice asking her to let him in.

She unlocked the main door, then went back to the sitting room, wondering what he wanted. Something to do with Daniel, probably, although she had no idea what. By the time he tapped on her door she had worked herself into such a state that it was hard to hide how nervous she felt as she let him in.

'I'm sorry to drop in on you without phoning first,' he said politely, following her into the sitting room.

'It's fine. Don't worry about it. I was just about to have a glass of wine—would you like one?'

'I'd better not. I'm driving so I'll give it a miss.'

'Tea, then—or coffee, perhaps?'

'No, thanks.' He flashed her a smile as he sat down on the sofa, but she could see how tense he looked, and it simply increased her own nervousness. 'I treated myself to dinner out tonight, and I think I might have over-indulged when it came to the pudding. My culinary repertoire doesn't run to puddings, so Daniel and I usually make do with fruit.'

'Far more healthy, although not so much fun,' she observed lightly, sitting down in the chair. She picked up her glass and took a sip of the wine to give herself something to do. She had no idea what he wanted, and wasn't sure what to do now that the usual pleasantries had been exchanged.

'I expect you're wondering what I'm doing here?'

Rose flushed when she realised how transparent she was. 'I was, actually,' she admitted, knowing it would be pointless to lie.

'To be honest, I'm not sure myself. I don't know what I hope to achieve by seeing you.'

She frowned when she heard the frustration in his voice. 'Are you still worried about Daniel? I understand if you are. I'd probably feel the same if our positions were reversed. All I can do is repeat that I won't do anything to hurt him.' Her voice caught. 'He's just as precious to me as he is to you, Owen, even though you find that difficult to believe.'

'I don't know what I believe any more!' he exploded. He ran a trembling hand over his face and she was shocked to see that his usual poise seemed to have deserted him.

'I never meant to cause you any problems,' she said urgently, willing him to believe her.

'So you keep saying. But the fact is that you *have* caused problems, and ones I never imagined either.'

He stood up abruptly and paced across the room. Rose could tell that he was struggling to regain control of himself and waited in silence. What could she say, anyway? That she didn't want to hurt him or Daniel? She'd told him that already, and it was true, too, so it was all the more painful to know that she was causing him so much anguish.

'Daniel told me about his father,' he said suddenly, swinging round. 'He also told me that your parents refused to help you after he was born.'

'That's right.' She wasn't sure where this was leading, but if it would help then she would tell him anything he wanted to know. She had nothing to hide, and the sooner he accepted that, the sooner he might learn to trust her.

It was surprising how important it seemed to gain his trust. Rose wasn't sure why it mattered so much and didn't waste her time speculating. She took a fortifying sip of her wine, then placed the glass carefully on the table.

'My father was very strict and he had stringent views about how people should behave. He was horrified when he found out I was pregnant. I think Mum might have come round to the idea eventually, but Dad was adamant and she chose to side with him. He refused to have anything to do with me after Daniel was born.'

'What about after you had Daniel adopted?' he asked, sitting down. 'Couldn't you have resolved your differences then?'

'I'm afraid not. I'd already done the unthinkable by having a baby, so the fact that I ended up having Daniel adopted made no difference. Oh, I did try phoning my parents at first, but they used to hang up as soon as they knew it was me so I gave up. Mum died ten years ago. We never spoke again after I left home, although I wrote to her occasionally. She never replied, though, so I'm not sure if she even read my letters.'

She bit her lip, trying not to let the painful memories overwhelm her. 'Dad never told me that she'd died, in fact. If it hadn't been for a friend from the village whom I'd kept in touch with I wouldn't have known. I went to her funeral, hoping I might be able to make my peace with him, but he refused to acknowledge me. Then, a few years ago, I heard he had Alzheimer's disease. He's in a nursing-home now and he has no idea who I am.'

'So you visit him?' he asked in surprise.

'Yes. I go every month,' she explained briefly. The fact that she paid the fees for her father's care had nothing to do with anyone but her—she certainly didn't want Owen thinking that she was trying to curry favour by telling him.

'Not many people would bother after what he did. I can't imagine how hard it must have been for you, Rose. Having to go through your pregnancy and Daniel's adoption all on your own.'

'It wasn't easy, but I did what I thought was best. I suppose if I'd been a bit more worldly-wise, none of it would have happened.'

'What do you mean?'

'I led a very sheltered life when I was growing up. Far more sheltered than most of my schoolfriends. Daniel's father was my first boyfriend, in fact. He'd just finished his finals at Oxford, and he and a group of friends had rented a house in the village where I lived so they could spend the summer surfing. He was such fun, and so different to everyone else I knew—I was totally smitten.'

'So it was a holiday romance?' he said gently.

'For him, yes. To me, it was a lot more than that. I fell head over heels in love with him and it never occurred to me that he didn't feel the same way.' She sighed. 'Which shows you how naïve I was, doesn't it?'

'You were just a kid, Rose—a young and very vulnerable teenager.'

'I was, although according to my father it was my lack of morals that got me into such a mess.'

'Hell!' He reached out and covered her hand with his. 'There's nothing immoral about falling in love, no matter what age you are. It's the most wonderful experience in the world when you find the right person.'

'Like when you met your wife?' she said softly, hoping he couldn't feel how her pulse was racing. His hand was so warm and strong that she wanted to hold onto it for ever and never let it go. If she had Owen to hold onto then she could cope with any problem, and the thought stunned her. It was a relief when he released her because she doubted if she could have pushed him away.

'Yes, just like when I met Laura. I fell in love with her the first time I saw her, although it took me a while to convince her I was serious.' His voice echoed with the memories and her heart contracted when she realised how painful it must be for him to think about what he'd lost.

'But you managed it in the end?'

'Oh, yes. I was determined, you see. She wasn't going to escape even though she kept putting all these obstacles in my path.' He glanced down and there was a wealth of emotion on his face when he looked up again. 'Laura knew she could never have a child of her own, you see. She'd had cancer before and the treatment had left her sterile. She was afraid our marriage wouldn't work if we couldn't have a family, but I talked her round.

'When we found out that we'd been accepted by the adoption agency we both cried for joy. And when we were allowed to adopt Daniel it felt as though life couldn't get any better. I think Laura loved him even more than she would have loved her own child because he was so special, so precious.'

'I'm so glad Daniel had you for his parents,' she said huskily. 'I could tell by the way he spoke about you the other day how much he loves you.'

'I love him, too, just as much,' he said simply. 'You gave Laura and me the most wonderful gift anyone can give another person. You gave us your son, Rose, and I thank you from the bottom of my heart for that. When Laura knew she was dying, she told me that having Daniel had given meaning to her life. Oh, she didn't want to die, and she fought until the end, but at least she died knowing that she'd left behind a son who would always love her.'

He buried his face in his hands, overcome by emotion. Rose went and knelt in front of him, putting her arms around him while he cried out all the pain and anguish. Tears were pouring down her own face, too, but her feelings didn't matter. It was Owen who was hurting, his pain that needed healing, and she would do everything she could to help him.

'Shh, it's all right. Everything's going to be fine,' she murmured, stroking his hair. The crisp black strands seemed to have a life of their own as they clung to her fingers and she felt a jolt of awareness run through her which she tried very hard to ignore.

Drawing his head into the crook of her neck, she murmured to him—soothing little sounds that had no meaning yet which obviously calmed him because she could feel some of the tension seeping from him. Encouraged by her success, her hand moved to the nape of his neck and she stroked that, too, wanting only to comfort him, yet she couldn't pretend that she didn't feel the surge of electricity that suddenly arced between them.

Owen raised his head and she could see the same awareness in his eyes that must have been in hers. He studied the tracks the tears had made on her cheeks and his voice was full of wonderment. 'You're crying for me?'

'Because you're hurting,' she whispered, unable to lie.

His eyes darkened and Rose held her breath. She had no idea what was going to happen next... Then all of a sudden he was bending towards her and she was reaching up to him until their mouths met in a kiss that seemed to strike to the very core of her being. It was as though the shape and taste of his lips had been imprinted in her mind the first time they'd kissed in the lift. Now all it needed was the touch of his mouth to unlock the memory so that she knew exactly what to do—how to tilt her head so that their lips could achieve the most perfect fusion.

Desire seared through her and she gasped, heard him gasp as well when he felt its effects, too. When she felt his tongue probing her lips she opened her mouth for him, and when she felt his hand caress her breast she didn't push it away. She wanted his touch just as much as she wanted his kiss, wanted it for herself and for him—to help him heal. Owen had given her a chance to show him the kind of person she really was, and she wasn't going to waste it on foolish doubts!

She cradled his face between her hands and kissed him back. She could feel the blood drumming through her veins, feel his blood beating with the same urgency as their passion soared. When he started to unbutton her blouse she helped him, not wanting anything to get in the way. His jacket came off next, then his tie, and all the time their mouths were melded together, giving and taking what they both so desperately needed. His shirt was a little more difficult—the buttons were so small and so difficult to unfasten. Rose murmured in frustration but she refused to be deterred. One, two, three…they slid out of the buttonholes and she sighed in triumph. Now there was just his belt to tackle…

Her hands went to his belt at the same moment as his went to the snap on her jeans. Owen drew back and grinned at her—a wolfish grin that was laced with male arrogance as well as desire. He knew that she wanted him, but there was no point pretending when he wanted her, too.

'Ladies first.'

'Thank you,' she retorted primly, reaching for the clasp at the end of the leather. Her fingers started to work the leather strap through the buckle, then paused when the telephone suddenly rang.

'Let it ring,' Owen ordered as he bent and plundered her mouth again. Rose didn't argue. She didn't want to. She just wanted to get rid of this wretched belt…

The answering-machine cut in, asking the caller to leave a message, and then Daniel's voice echoed around the room. 'Hi, Rose. Obviously you're not in, so I'll try again tomorrow. I was hoping we might be able to meet up again on Saturday. Oh, it's Daniel, by the way. I nearly forgot. Bye!'

The line went dead, and in the silence Rose could hear her heart beating. She was already prepared when Owen dragged himself away from her and stood up.

'I'm sorry,' he said hoarsely, tucking his shirt back into the waistband of his trousers with angry, jerky movements.

Rose felt sick as she stumbled to her feet. They had done nothing wrong but she could tell he didn't believe that from the way he refused to look at her.

'There's nothing to apologise for.'

'Maybe not in your eyes but there is in mine!'

He snatched his jacket off the sofa and dragged it on. His face was taut with anger but she knew it wasn't aimed at her. She wished it was, because this was so much worse. He was angry with himself for lowering his guard. In his heart he still saw her as the enemy, and it was unbearably painful to know how he felt after what they had just shared.

'Then I must apologise, too.' She stared back at him, refusing to let him see how wounded she felt. 'If I forced you to compromise your principles, Owen, I'm very sorry.'

A wash of colour ran up his face, but he didn't attempt to use the excuse she had offered him. 'You didn't make me do anything I didn't want to do. The fault was mine, and I shall make sure it doesn't happen again.'

'And is that what you decided last time after you kissed me?' she taunted, hating herself for hitting back at him yet unable to stop. Why wouldn't he accept that she didn't want to harm him? Surely he should have known that after what had just happened?

'Yes. I made up my mind that I would never put myself in this position again, but obviously I underestimated how vulnerable I am where you are concerned.' His gaze grazed over her and she flinched when she saw the self-contempt it held. That he should feel such self-loathing reflected on her. 'You are a very beautiful woman, Rose, and I won't deny that I want you, but I won't put my needs before Daniel's happiness.'

'So you still don't trust me? Is that what you're saying?'

'I don't know you well enough to trust you.' Just for a moment his assurance wavered, as though he doubted the truth of what he was saying, then he managed to collect himself. 'I'm sorry. I should never have come here tonight.'

He didn't say anything else as he left the room. Rose heard the front door opening and closing again after he left but she didn't move. She stood right where she was, listening to her own heart beating in the silence. Closing her eyes, she let herself remember the taste of Owen's mouth, the scent of his skin, the texture of his hair; let herself create some memories. That was all she would have now: memories. He wouldn't kiss her again, wouldn't compromise Daniel's safety by letting himself feel anything for her. He wouldn't allow himself to enjoy what they could have had together because, despite what he thought, *she* knew they could have had something special.

He wouldn't do anything to make this situation better because he didn't trust her, and nothing had ever hurt as much as knowing that. Nothing ever would. Owen didn't trust her and there wasn't a thing she could do to convince him that he was wrong about her.

CHAPTER TEN

'I SUGGEST you all concentrate on what you're supposed to be doing. There's no excuse for a mistake like this. A patient very nearly died!'

Owen strode out of Resus, ignoring the silence that followed in his wake. The day was turning into a disaster. It was still only ten a.m. and already they'd lost a patient. It was only through the grace of God that they hadn't lost a second one, too. There was no room in the department for people who couldn't make the right decisions and act on them.

He turned to Suzanne, hardening his heart when he saw the misery on his registrar's face. 'How many times have you seen a patient admitted with breathing difficulties?' he demanded, refusing to think about the real reason for his bad temper that day.

His expression darkened when Suzanne murmured that she had no idea how many people she'd seen.

'And that's because it's one of the most frequent problems we encounter. People stop breathing for any number of reasons. Pneumothorax, haemothorax, an obstruction in the airway… You've seen it happen time after time, so why did you need me to tell you what the problem was? Why didn't you diagnose it and begin the appropriate treatment?'

'I just worry in case I've got it wrong…' She tailed off unhappily and Owen sighed.

'None of us is infallible, Suzanne. The trick is to minimise the risks through correct diagnosis. You knew the patient had no air entry on the left side. You also knew that the odds on it being a pneumothorax or a haemothorax were greatly increased because of the nature of his injuries—broken ribs and severe bruising to the chest. Yet you still needed my say-so before you went ahead and requested an X-ray. That delay nearly cost him his life.'

'I'm sorry. I wish I was more confident, but I'm always afraid of doing the wrong thing in the heat of the moment,' she admitted.

'Then maybe you should decide if you're cut out for this work. You're a good doctor, Suzanne, and far more capable than you give yourself credit for. But if you can't make on-the-spot decisions then you should think about a change of direction.'

He left it at that. It was up to Suzanne to decide what she in-tended to do. The rest of the team had left Resus now that the patient was on his way to Theatre, so he went to the nursing station to see if there was anything urgent that needed his at-tention. Rose was there, talking to Angie, but she cut short their conversation when she saw him approaching.

Angie raised a questioning brow as she watched Rose hurry away.

'Am I safe, or should I follow Rose's example and find somewhere to hide?'

'You're perfectly safe,' he replied shortly, checking the whiteboard. All the cubicles were full and there was someone in the treatment room as well—an average day, in fact.

'Good. I don't fancy being torn off a strip. I value my hide too much,' Angie declared, picking up the board rubber to re-move the last patient's details from the resus slot. 'Mind you, I'm not too sure what Rose thinks she's done to incur your wrath.'

'Nothing.' Owen shrugged when he saw the sceptical look

the charge nurse gave him. 'I haven't said a word to her all morning.'

'I know. Odd, isn't it? You've bitten off everyone else's head but you've left Rose alone. It makes me wonder what she's got that we haven't.'

Angie bustled away before he could deny that Rose had been singled out for special treatment. However, it was worrying to know that people were speculating about the way he behaved towards her. He would have to be more careful in future, treat her the same way he treated everyone else…

Oh, yes, a small inner voice jeered. So he'd be just as grumpy with Rose as he was with the rest of the staff? He wouldn't even *think* about the fact that he'd kissed her last night *and* enjoyed it?

Owen cursed under his breath. He knew there was little hope of him sticking to the decision. Rose wasn't just one of his staff—that was the trouble. She was more than that, a lot more, far more than he wanted her to be. He might regret his lapse but it didn't mean he would forget how wonderful it had felt when he'd kissed her, so help him!

Rose made a point of keeping out of Owen's way for the rest of the morning. Fortunately, Angie asked her to work the cubicles, so she was able to avoid him until it was time for her lunch-break. She went to the canteen with Ellen and Sharon. The other nurses seemed to have accepted her now, and she had to admit that she enjoyed not feeling like an outsider for once. Angie had dropped several hints about her taking a permanent post in the department, but she'd had to reject the idea. Not only would it be financially impractical to give up her agency job, there was the problem of Owen's reaction. And after last night she knew how much he would hate the idea.

'So there you are! I've been looking everywhere for you lot.'

Rose looked up in surprise when Rob appeared. 'What are you doing here? I thought you were on nights this week.'

'And so I am. I dragged myself out of bed just so I could bring a little joy and happiness into your lives.' He pulled over a chair and sat down. 'I'm having a party on Saturday and you're all invited!'

Rose laughed as everyone cheered. 'Sounds like a popular idea. What's the big occasion?'

'There isn't one. I just feel like having a bit of fun after working my fingers to the bone on night duty... Hang on a second. Didn't you say something about it being your birthday this week?' He grinned when she reluctantly admitted that it was. 'That's it, then—we're going to celebrate your birthday. So that means you'll be my guest of honour!'

'Oh, no, really, I couldn't,' Rose protested.

'Of course you could!' He wagged his finger at her. 'Don't be such a spoilsport. I'll cancel the party if you don't agree to come.'

'That's blackmail!' she accused him, as everyone laughed.

'I know,' he agreed without a trace of shame. 'So does that mean you'll come?'

Rose groaned. 'I don't have much choice, do I?'

Rob promised to let them have the details before Saturday and left. As soon as he'd gone everyone started discussing what they were going to wear for the party, and by the time they'd sorted it out it was time to return to work.

The afternoon was even busier than the morning had been, although thankfully there were no more disasters. News of the party soon spread and several people offered their congratulations when they found out it was Rose's birthday. The only person who didn't say anything was Owen. He remained aloof from the proceedings, although what had she expected? It didn't make any difference to him if she was celebrating her birthday.

Owen tried not to think about the forthcoming party for the remainder of the week, but it was difficult to ignore what was happening when everyone was talking about it. Rob had put up a poster in the staffroom, inviting them all along, so it wasn't as though he could claim ignorance of the event. When Angie asked him if he was going, he told her very firmly that he had made other plans. It wasn't true because he wasn't planning on doing anything. He just knew it would be a mistake to spend any more time with Rose after the last disastrous occasion.

Saturday was showery, the rain drenching the city streets. Daniel had arranged to see Rose again that afternoon, so Owen was left to his own devices. He spent the time pottering around the house and trying not to think about what they were doing, but it was impossible. He kept picturing them having fun together and it was very unsettling to be left on the outside.

Daniel was very buoyed up when he came home, and Owen's spirits sank even further as he listened to him praising Rose to the hilt. According to Daniel, she could do no wrong and it worried him to know how attached to her Daniel was becoming in view of what he'd heard about her reluctance to make a long-term commitment. If anything happened to ruin their new-found relationship, he would be left to pick up the pieces. He couldn't bear to imagine what such a rejection might do to his son.

The thought plagued him all through dinner and he knew that he wouldn't be able to rest until he'd spoken to Rose about it. When Daniel announced that he'd invited some friends over to listen to some music, it seemed like the ideal opportunity. Owen certainly didn't want to discuss the issue with her at work, neither did he intend to risk another visit to her home so he would drop into the party and have a word with her there.

The festivities were in full swing when he arrived. Rob had taped a note on the front door, telling people to go straight in, so he followed the instructions, wincing when his ears were assaulted by the sound of music being played at full volume. Angie was sitting on the stairs with her boyfriend and she did a double-take when she saw him.

'I thought you couldn't come?'

'Change of plans,' he explained briefly. He held up a carrier bag. 'Where's Rob? I've got a couple of bottles for him.'

'He's gone upstairs to invite his neighbours so they don't complain about the noise.' Angie pointed along the hall. 'Drinks are in the kitchen, so you can leave them in there.'

'Thanks.'

Owen made his way through the crowd that had gathered in the hall. There were a lot of people there from the hospital and most looked surprised to see him. It made him realise how long it had been since he'd socialised with his colleagues.

The crush in the kitchen was even worse than in the hall, and he had to wait until a few people came out before he could go in. His heart seemed to leap right up into his throat when he spotted Rose standing behind a makeshift bar. She'd dressed up especially for the occasion and he couldn't drag his eyes away from her as he made his way to the front of the queue. She looked so beautiful in a sparkly little green top with her blonde hair curling around her face that it would have needed a harder heart than his not to feel anything. Just for a second he allowed himself the pleasure of looking at her before she glanced up and saw him.

'I brought these as a contribution to the festivities,' he said hurriedly, handing her the carrier bag.

'Oh…thanks. That's really kind of you.' She took the bag from him, fumbling a little as they passed it over the table so that he had to grab hold of the bottom to stop her dropping it.

'Thank you,' she murmured, avoiding his eyes as she placed the bottles on the worktop behind her. He saw her shoulders straighten before she turned, and something warm and tender seemed to flower inside him when he realised that she was strugging to get a grip on herself. In that moment he realised something that he should have realised sooner—that Rose was experiencing just as much difficulty sorting out her feelings as he was.

The thought made him gasp and she looked at him in concern. 'Are you all right?'

'Fine. Just a bit overwhelmed by all the noise,' he said quickly, trying not to make too much of the fact that she seemed worried about him. It was impossible to stop his mind spinning off on yet another track: Rose cared about him after the way he'd treated her?

It was just too much to take in. He dredged up a smile, needing to ease himself out of a situation he wasn't ready to deal with. 'I wouldn't mind a beer if you're on bar duty, though.'

'Of course.' She expertly flipped the cap off a bottle of beer and handed it to him. 'I'm afraid we've run out of glasses.'

'Not to worry.' He took a swallow out of the bottle, then looked round when someone behind him asked for a glass of wine. There was quite a queue building up again and he realised that he couldn't keep hogging her attention. 'I'll go and join the fray. Thanks for this. I'll catch up with you later.'

He left the kitchen and made his way into the sitting room. Charlie was acting as DJ. He waved when Owen passed him, heading for the corner where he could wait until Rose had finished her bar duties. All he wanted was a quick word with her about Daniel, then he would leave, but she didn't appear to be in any hurry to join the other guests.

Charlie put a slow track on the deck and people started to pair off. Owen was about to refuse when Ellen asked him to dance, then suddenly decided that he might as well make the effort to enjoy himself, seeing that he was there. Rob had reappeared and was dancing with Suzanne, their two heads close together. Owen felt a little stab of envy as he watched them. It had been a long time since he'd held a woman in his arms and let the music carry him away.

The track ended so he thanked Ellen and had started to go back to the corner when he realised that Rose had come into the room. He wasn't even aware that he was moving until he found himself standing in front of her. 'Dance with me?' he said softly.

'If you're sure it's what you want?' she said, looking up at him with solemn eyes.

Owen didn't say a word as he took hold of her hand because he wasn't sure about anything any more. He led her to the centre of the room and took her in his arms, and it felt like a homecoming. When someone lowered the lights it was as though the very last of his defences had been lowered, too.

He drew her to him as they swayed in time to the seductive rhythm. He could feel her body brushing against his as they moved, smell the fragrance of her hair, and senses which had been reawakened that night at her flat came surging back to life. Bending, he rested his cheek against her temple, allowing himself the licence to enjoy the moment. Maybe he was making another mistake, but he couldn't believe that what felt so right could be wrong. He was trusting his instincts now, and his instincts were telling him that he had nothing to be scared about, that Rose wouldn't hurt him.

The music came to an end and someone turned on the lights. Owen smiled wryly when everyone booed. 'I know how they feel.'

'Do you?'

He could hear the uncertainty in her voice and his heart contracted when he realised that she had every reason to doubt him. He had behaved very badly towards her and he had a lot of ground to make up if he hoped to gain her trust.

'Yes. I enjoyed dancing with you, Rose. I didn't want to stop.' His voice was very deep and he felt the shudder that passed through her before she quickly stepped back.

'I'd better check that everyone's got a drink.'

'I thought it was supposed to be your party?' he parried, reluctant to let her leave him.

'It is…well, partly. But I offered to help and I don't want to let Rob down.'

'He doesn't look too bothered to me,' he observed dryly, glancing over at where Rob and Suzanne were standing, still entwined in each other's arms. They seemed unaware that the music had stopped, something that was causing great amusement amongst the other guests.

'Maybe not, but I'd prefer to do what I said I would,' she said, edging away.

'I understand.' He took a deep breath but the truth had to be acknowledged. 'You aren't someone who goes back on your word, are you, Rose?'

'No. I always try to keep my promises.'

She looked into his eyes and he saw the dawning hope in hers. Reaching out, he touched her cheek. 'I think we need to talk, don't we?'

'Yes. But not here. It's too noisy.'

'It is.' He gave her a slow smile, surprised at how easy it was now that he'd taken the first, difficult step towards trusting her. 'We'll leave it till later…after the party is over.'

'I'd like that.'

She smiled at him, then hurried from the room. Owen let her go because he was confident that they would have that talk and that it would resolve a lot of problems, too. Now that he could see Rose for the person she really was he was no longer afraid of the harm she might cause. Rose wasn't a threat to his son. She was a warm and caring woman. A woman he could very easily learn to love.

'Thank you all so much. I never expected this!'

Rose blinked back her tears. Unknown to her, the staff had organised a collection and bought her a birthday cake with the proceeds, and she was really touched by everyone's generosity. Coming on top of what Owen had said to her earlier in the evening, it was little wonder that she was feeling so emotional.

Her eyes sought him out of the crowd and her pulse leapt when she saw him watching her from the far side of the room. Even from that distance she could see the warmth in his eyes, and it felt wonderful to see it after the way he usually looked at her.

'Come on, now, no weeping all over the cake and melting the icing! We all want a slice, don't we, guys?'

Rose laughed when Rob handed her a scalpel. She was just about to cut into the cake when Suzanne stopped her.

'Wait! You've got to blow out the candles and make a wish first!'

'Oops! I nearly forgot.' Rose took a deep breath and blew out all the candles, shaking her head when Suzanne demanded to know what she'd wished for. 'Sorry, that's a secret.'

Everyone clapped as she cut into the cake, then Charlie put another record on the deck and people started to drift away. Rose took the cake into the kitchen and found a proper knife to finish slicing it up. She glanced round when she realised that someone had followed her and felt her pulse leap when she saw Owen standing in the doorway.

'How about we make our escape after you've finished doing that?'

'Fine by me.' She quickly divided the cake into portions, then wiped her hands on a teatowel. 'I'll just tell Rob that I'm leaving first.'

'I wouldn't bother, if I were you. He and Suzanne seemed to be rather busy when I last saw them.' He raised a meaningful brow, and she laughed.

'I won't interrupt them, then.'

Rose fetched her coat and they left the flat together. Although it was gone midnight, there were a lot of people about when they reached the street. Owen frowned as he glanced along the road.

'I'm almost sure you can get down to the Embankment from here. Fancy a stroll by the river to wind down?'

'It sounds good to me,' she agreed readily.

It was just a ten-minute walk to the Embankment, and neither of them said anything on the way. Rose sensed that he was waiting until they were on their own before he raised the subject that was uppermost in both their minds. They walked down the steps and stopped by the safety rail, watching the Thames flowing past beneath them. There was an almost full moon that night and the water shimmered silver in its light.

'I think I owe you an apology, Rose. I've behaved very badly towards you.'

Owen's tone was quiet, in keeping with the mood, and she tried to match it. 'You did what you thought was right.'

'But that doesn't excuse the way I've treated you.' He turned to her and his face looked stern in the moonlight. 'I judged you without even attempting to get to know you, and that was wrong of me.'

'You were worried about Daniel,' she protested, hating to hear him blame himself.

'I was, but I never tried to see the situation from your side. I just assumed that meeting you would be detrimental to him.' He paused, and she could hear the pain in his voice when he carried on. 'My fears weren't solely on his behalf either. I was worried in case meeting you would affect how he felt about me. I…I couldn't bear to lose him.'

'Daniel loves you! I couldn't take away what you two have even if I wanted to.'

'I know that now, but I wasn't thinking straight.' He smiled tightly and she could see the emotion on his face. 'I was scared of losing him as well as Laura. I wouldn't have had anything worth living for then. I suppose it was the fear of being left on my own that made me behave so irrationally, especially after I was told that you are someone who avoids commitment.'

'Who told you that?' she exclaimed, and he shrugged.

'Just someone who knew you when you worked at the Royal. I'm sorry. I shouldn't have been listening to gossip.'

'I understand why you wanted to find out more about me,' she said quietly, turning to stare at the river. 'And I suppose it's true. I have always avoided getting too involved with anyone.'

'Is there a reason for that?'

'Yes.' She took a quick breath, but there was no way that she was going to lie to him now. 'I never wanted to take a chance on falling in love again after what I did.'

'After what you did?' he repeated uncertainly.

'I gave Daniel away, and I've had to live with the guilt of that for all these years.'

'But you did it to help him! You did it so he would have a better life than you could provide for him at the time!'

'Yes, but—'

'There are no buts, Rose,' he said firmly. 'You did what you thought was right for Daniel and you have nothing to blame yourself for.'

'And neither do you. You were only trying to protect Daniel.'

'Was I? Or was I trying to protect my own interests more?'

'I don't believe that,' she said fiercely, grasping his hand. 'The same as I don't believe that Daniel would ever turn his back on you. You're his father, Owen, and he loves you very much.'

'And you're his mother, Rose. You're the reason he exists. If it hadn't been for your bravery in giving birth to him, I wouldn't have had the joy of watching him grow up.'

He turned her hand over so that he could lift it to his mouth. Rose closed her eyes when she felt him press his lips to her palm. The kiss was both a tender acknowledgement of her status as Daniel's mother and the most erotic stimulant she'd ever experienced. Already she could feel her blood heating, her body quickening, her desire growing, and it was a shock to feel the enormity of her need.

She had never felt like this before—eager and hungry for his kisses, wanting everything he could give her yet wanting to give him even more. What did it mean? Was it possible that she was falling in love with him, the father of her son? And, if it was true, what effect would it have on Daniel?

She knew how vulnerable Daniel was. He was still grieving for Laura and he might not take kindly to the idea of his father having a relationship with his birth mother. Was she prepared to take that risk, to *harm* him in any way at all?

A cold chill enveloped her. She knew the answer to that question without having to think about it. She would never hurt Daniel, certainly wouldn't put her needs before his. Even though she knew this attraction she felt for Owen was something very special, she would never jeopardise her son's happiness. If she had to choose between father and son then she would choose Daniel, even though her heart ached at the thought of what she might be giving up.

CHAPTER ELEVEN

Owen could sense Rose's withdrawal even though he had no idea what he'd done to prompt it. When she removed her hand from his he didn't try to stop her.

He turned to stare at the river, wondering what had happened to change the mood. He wasn't stupid—he'd felt her response when he'd kissed her palm. She'd been as aroused by the tender caress as he had been so what had made her draw back? Was he going too fast for her, trying to change the direction of their relationship too quickly?

His heart raced as he considered which way he wanted it to go, before he quickly erased the thought. He wasn't going to spoil things by rushing when he had all the time in the world to get this right. He turned to her, deliberately keeping his tone light because he could see how troubled she looked.

'It's beautiful down here at this time of the night, isn't it? It's the best time to really appreciate the city.'

'Yes, it is.' She gave him a tentative smile in return but he could see the worry in her eyes and it was all he could do not to ask her what was wrong. However, he'd made up his mind that he wasn't going to rush her and he would stick to that— unlike all the other decisions he'd made recently.

His stomach clenched as he recalled all the things he'd sworn he would do. Keeping Rose out of Daniel's life had been at the very top of his list but he'd not achieved it. He'd also failed to keep his distance from her, too. It was as though he no sooner made up his mind than he changed it again, and it wasn't like him to vacillate. All of a sudden he was beset by doubts again. Was he right to make such a drastic switch of direction, or did he need to think things through before he went any further?

'I'd better go home. It's late and I have to get up early in the morning.'

'Of course.'

Owen straightened, not sorry to have a reason to bring the evening to an end. There was no point risking everything on a whim. 'I'll see if I can find us a taxi,' he offered, closing his mind to the insidious little voice which was mocking his attempts to behave sensibly. *The way he felt about Rose wasn't a whim! He was just backpedalling because he was scared of getting hurt...*

'Ah, there's one now.' He ran up the steps and flagged down the cab, using actions to blot out the taunts. Rose followed him up to the road, but she didn't get into the taxi when he opened the door.

'You take this one and I'll find another one. After all, we're going in completely different directions.'

'I'm not leaving you here on your own,' he replied firmly. 'I can drop you off first and then carry on home.'

'Well, if you're sure...'

She hesitated a moment longer, then got into the cab. Owen told the driver her address, then climbed in after her and closed the door. He wasn't sure why she seemed so reluctant to let him see her home.

Unless she was afraid that he might expect to be invited in?

Blood rushed to his head at the thought and it was the devil of a job to calm himself down. However, there was no way that he was going to be spending the night in her bed so he'd better put that idea right out of his mind!

They made desultory conversation as the taxi drove across the city. Rose seemed loath to engage in any talk of a personal nature and he was wary of saying something out of turn. It was a relief to both of them when the cab drew up outside the block of flats where she lived.

'Thank you for the lift,' she said politely, reaching for the doorhandle.

'Don't mention it.' He summoned a smile, wishing the evening didn't have to end this way even though he knew it was safer. He needed a bit more time to make sure that he knew what he was doing—for his sake as well as for Daniel's. 'I'll see you at work next week.'

'I expect so.'

One last smile and then she got out. Owen glanced back as the cab sped away but she had already gone inside. He turned around, fighting the urge to ask the driver to go back. He mustn't make the mistake of rushing into something he could regret, he reminded himself sternly. However, he couldn't shake off the feeling that he was leaving part of himself behind as the taxi drove along the road. Rose had taken a bit of his heart with him when she'd left.

Rose had planned on visiting her father the following day, so she got up early to catch the train. She'd spent a restless night, and when she had slept her dreams had been full of Owen. She knew that she was on the verge of falling in love with him and the idea scared her after what had happened all those years ago. However, her biggest fear was the effect it might have on Daniel. That was why it was so important that she made the right decision.

She spent a couple of hours at the nursing-home, then travelled back to London. Although her father had no idea who she was, he seemed to enjoy her visits and that made the long journey worthwhile. It was after seven when she let herself into the flat and there was a message from Daniel on her answering-machine, suggesting they meet for lunch the following Saturday.

Once again he'd chosen somewhere in the city where they could meet, and it seemed to point towards the fact that he didn't want her visiting his home. He wanted to keep his home life separate from her, so maybe she should take that as a warning of how he would feel if she became involved with his father. When she went to bed that night Rose was more unsure than ever. The only thing she was certain about was that she wouldn't do anything to hurt Daniel.

The main topic of conversation at work the following morning seemed to be Rob and Suzanne. There was a great deal of speculation about whether the two registrars were now officially an 'item'. Rose laughed when she was asked for her views.

'Pass! I'm the world's worst when it comes to pairing people off. Why do you think I'm still single?'

'Not because of a lack of offers, I don't imagine.' Angie gave her a speaking look as she stowed her coat in her locker. 'I saw you and Owen leaving the party together, so is there anything you want to tell us?'

'Of course not!' She flushed when everyone laughed. 'Honestly, there's nothing going on between me and Owen. I don't even like him!' she added in a desperate attempt to put a stop to any gossip.

'Excuse me. Can I have a word with you, Angie?'

She swung round when a familiar voice interrupted their conversation, and her heart sank when she realised that Owen had come into the room without them noticing. She couldn't imagine what he must have made of her comment, but she saw the sympathetic looks the rest of the staff gave her as they left.

Rose followed them out and went straight to Reception to fetch her first patient. She would have to apologise to him later for what she'd said. Hopefully, he would understand why she'd felt it necessary to squash any rumours. Her heart lurched, because she and Owen didn't have a good track record when it came to explaining things, did they?

Owen knew it was ridiculous to feel hurt because of what he'd overheard but he couldn't help it. Rose had stated quite categorically that she didn't like him and it had been painful to hear. He tried to put it out of his mind as he ran through the previous week's statistics with Angie. A couple of times they had exceeded the allotted waiting time and he knew there would be questions from management when they saw the figures.

'It happened when you were dealing with that major incident,' the charge nurse explained. 'We sent some patients home but a lot of people decided to wait. The ones who stayed took us over the time limit.'

'Right, that's fine. So long as I know the reason then I'll be able to sort it out. Waiting-time limits sound fine in principle, but they can't always be adhered to.'

'I expect there'll be some grumbling from on high but we did our best,' Angie assured him, then rushed on. 'I'm sorry about what happened earlier. It was my fault because I was teasing Rose about you and her disappearing together on Saturday night. I expect that's why she said what she did—I'd backed her into a corner.'

'I'm sure you're right,' he agreed coolly, making it clear that he didn't intend to discuss the matter. Fortunately, Angie took the hint, but it was unsettling to know that the staff had been talking about him and Rose. Maybe it wasn't a bad thing that she'd claimed not to like him if it had stopped the gossip, he thought.

There was no time to dwell on it, however, because just then Sharon knocked on the office door and told him they had a casualty being rushed in. He went straight to Resus and was ready to receive the patient when the paramedics arrived. The casualty was a thirteen-year-old boy called Andrew Davenport. He'd been walking to school when some older boys had attacked him and stolen his mobile phone. He'd been stabbed in the back and he'd lost a lot of blood.

'Hello, Andrew, I'm Dr Gallagher.' Owen introduced himself as they lifted the boy onto a bed. 'I'm going to check you over and make you more comfortable.'

'I didn't do anything,' the boy whispered, his eyes welling with tears. 'They just stabbed me when I said I wouldn't give them my phone.'

'Let's not worry about that now. It's more important that we get you sorted out.'

Owen glanced up as Angie rattled out the boy's BP, heart-rate and sats levels. Andrew had been put on a drip by the paramedics and at the moment that was compensating for all the blood he'd lost. If more than ten per cent of the total volume of blood was lost from the circulatory system, a patient would lapse into shock, and that was why they were put on a drip. However, it was only a temporary measure, and the boy would need a blood transfusion soon.

'Can you cross-match him for three litres of blood?' he instructed. 'And we'll need some O neg while we're waiting.'

'My blood group is B positive,' Andrew whispered.

'Is it indeed?' Owen grinned as he moved around the bed so he could examine the stab wound. He nodded to Angie and she helped him roll Andrew over onto his side so Owen could see what he was doing. 'I'm impressed. It's not often we get a patient who knows his own blood group.'

'I asked the doctor what it was when I had to have a blood test last year,' Andrew explained.

'I see. Are you interested in medicine, then?' Owen carefully probed the wound. It was roughly one centimetre across and appeared slightly wider at one end than the other. He guessed it had been made with some sort of small kitchen knife—like a paring knife, for instance.

'Yes. I want to be a doctor when I leave school.'

'Excellent! We need bright young lads like you.'

He glanced round when Suzanne appeared, and nodded when she offered to help. She'd been very subdued since he'd told her off and he couldn't help noticing how much more confident she seemed that day. It was amazing the effect love could have, he thought wryly.

But he couldn't think about that now when he had a job to do. He gently explored the area around the stab wound, frowning in consternation when he realised how swollen it was. If he wasn't mistaken there was heavy internal bleeding, and that pointed towards there being damage to the major organs. The knife had entered the body near the left kidney, so there could be damage to the kidney or to the spleen, which lay just above it. Either event was potentially life-threatening, so he called Beth over and asked her to take X-rays.

Five minutes later Owen had his answer, and he sighed when he saw the shadow on the X-ray which indicated heavy bleeding in the area. He looked round when Suzanne came to take a look. 'Doesn't look too good, does it?'

'Looks like the kidney has been damaged,' she said, leaning closer. 'There might even be some damage to the spleen—maybe it was nicked when the blade entered.'

'You could be right.' He checked the screen again and nodded. 'We'll send him straight to Theatre, if you could do the honours. I don't want there to be any delay with this one.'

'Okey-dokey!'

Suzanne hurried away and he smiled to himself when he saw there was a definite bounce in her step that day. If it was love making such an improvement to her attitude then long might it last!

'Excuse me.'

'Sorry.' He stepped aside so Rose could put some soiled dressings in the bio-hazard container, feeling his heart sink. Love wasn't always all positives and no negatives, though. That was why he needed to think everything through very carefully: him and Rose; him and Daniel; him, Daniel and Rose—the permutations were endless. It wasn't going to be easy to work out what he should do, and he grimaced as he went to tell Andrew that he would be going to Theatre. Trusting his instincts wasn't an option in this instance, because they would definitely lead him astray!

Rose wasn't surprised that Owen seemed to be avoiding her. After what he'd overheard her saying that morning it would have been surprising if he'd sought her out. However, it didn't lessen her desire to explain the circumstances that had led to that unfortunate remark. She bided her time, and when she saw him going into the office she hurried after him.

'Can I have a word with you?' she asked, glancing over her shoulder to check that nobody was watching.

'Sure.' He opened the office door and ushered her inside. 'If it's about this morning—' he began.

'It is. I'm really sorry you overheard that, Owen. I don't know what you must have thought…'

'I didn't think anything.' He shrugged dismissively. 'I've got better things to do with my time than worry about what people think of me.'

'I'm sure you have.' Rose summoned a smile, but she had to admit that she was surprised by his attitude. He didn't seem to care how she really felt, and it was a shock after what had happened on Saturday night.

Heat flowed through as she recalled how he had kissed her palm. It had been such a sensual kiss that she could still feel the imprint his lips had made on her skin. She curled her fingers over the spot, letting the tingle spread up her arm. Owen had cared what she'd thought on Saturday night, and she couldn't believe the situation could have changed that much in the interim.

'Is that it, then? There was nothing else you wanted to see me about?'

Rose blinked when she heard a definite hint of impatience in his voice. Obviously he wasn't keen to prolong the conversation. 'No. I didn't want you getting the wrong idea, that's all.'

'I didn't.' He treated her to a decidedly impersonal smile as he opened the door. 'Thanks, Rose, but there's no need to worry. I'm not going to lose any sleep over it, I promise you.'

'Good.' Rose fixed a matching smile to her mouth and left. She wasn't sure what was going on but she certainly wasn't going to beg him to listen to her. If he was happy to dismiss the incident then she was, too.

She went back to work and spent the rest of the day dealing with her patients' problems. Fractures, cuts, head injuries—it always amazed her what people could do to themselves. It was a busy day and, apart from her break times, she worked non-stop. She knew that she'd achieved a lot by the end of the day, but as she made her way to the bus stop after her shift was over she felt none of her usual sense of satisfaction at a job well done. There was a niggling feeling inside her that one problem hadn't been resolved, and that problem was Owen.

What *was* going on?

Owen ended up working late even though he hadn't planned on doing so. They were supposed to be getting agency cover that night, but the registrar who'd been booked to work for them never turned up. He got onto the agency but the office was closed and there was just an answering-machine to field any queries.

He left a terse message and hung up, sighing when he realised that it was down to him to sort out the mess. Rob and Suzanne had wafted out of the building on a cloud of euphoria half an hour before. They were planning on spending a cosy evening together and he didn't have the heart to ask one of them to come back to work. He ended up phoning a colleague from another department and called in a few favours, then went to find Charlie and explained that he would work the first half of the shift and that Lawrence Banks, one of the general surgical team, had agreed to cover the rest. Devinder was on duty that night so he would be there as well.

Charlie laughed. 'You must be going soft in your old age, Owen. It's not like you to put the registrars' love lives before their jobs.'

'The mood that pair are in it's probably safer for the patients to keep them well away from here,' he retorted pithily.

'Now, now, no sour grapes, please,' Charlie said reprovingly. 'There's no need to spoil a beautiful gesture.'

'I suppose not.' Owen laughed. 'And it was a bit unfair of me to say that. Suzanne seems to have taken on a new lease of life thanks to this budding romance.'

'Some of Rob's cockiness must be rubbing off on her.' Charlie grinned. 'The power of love, eh? It makes you feel all warm and tingly inside to witness it, doesn't it?'

'Speak for yourself!' he retorted, not wanting the charge nurse to know that the comment had touched a nerve. Maybe love did make one feel all warm and tingly, but it also caused a lot of problems. He was very much aware that he hadn't sorted out his own situation yet.

There was no time to worry about it thankfully because they had a waiting room full of patients. He went into the office and phoned Daniel to warn him he was having to stay late, then got on with the job. Devinder was getting into his stride now that he was gaining more experience, so Owen was able to leave him to deal with the less complicated cases, but there were still a lot of people he needed to see himself. By the time the queue had been whittled down it was almost ten o'clock and he was flagging.

He told Charlie to call Lawrence if he got stuck and left, grateful that the drive home was much less stressful at that time of the night. By the time he turned into his driveway he was ready to drop. Supper, drink, shower and bed, he promised himself as he let himself into the house. And maybe he would even delete a couple items from that list. He was too tired to be hungry and too worn out to make himself a drink, so shower and bed might be the best options.

He went upstairs and tapped on Daniel's door to tell him he was home. The boy was lying on his bed, reading a lurid-looking thriller that Owen guessed wasn't part of his official college reading list. He forbore to say anything, though, because Daniel needed a break the same as everyone else did.

'Did you see Rose today?'

Owen was about to wend his weary way along the landing when Daniel shot the question at him, and his heart bumped as he stopped. 'Yes,' he said carefully, hoping the turmoil he was feeling wasn't apparent in his tone.

'Was she OK?'

He shrugged, wondering where the conversation was leading. 'She seemed to be. Why are you asking?'

'Oh, no reason, really. I was just wondering, that's all.' Daniel paused and Owen could tell there was something bothering him.

'Are you worried about what's happening between you and Rose?' he asked gently. 'It's been a big thing, you meeting her like this, so it's understandable if you have some concerns.'

'I don't...well, not really.' Daniel shrugged, making a brave stab at feigning indifference. 'I just don't want her to think that she *has* to keep on seeing me if it isn't what she really wants to do.'

'I'm sure Rose would tell you if she didn't want your meetings to continue,' he said firmly, even though his stomach had started churning.

That was something else he needed to take into account, wasn't it? What would happen if Rose decided at some point in the future that she'd had enough of motherhood? If he'd involved her in their lives, it would make the situation even more difficult—for him and for Daniel. He couldn't bear to imagine Daniel's pain if he grew used to having Rose around and she rejected him. He couldn't bear to imagine his *own* pain if she did the same thing!

He wished Daniel goodnight and went into the bathroom. Stripping off his clothes, he turned on the shower, then stood there with the water pounding down on his head. He and Daniel had had their hearts broken when Laura had died. Was he prepared to risk it happening a second time?

CHAPTER TWELVE

IT WAS Rose's last week at St Anne's, and she was surprised by how sad she felt about leaving. She'd worked at other hospitals for equally long periods but she'd never felt this way before. It was partly because the staff had been so friendly, but mainly because of Owen. She didn't want to leave him, especially when there were still so many unanswered questions about the way he had behaved towards her since the previous Saturday.

Tuesday, Wednesday and Thursday came and went, and Owen avoided her. Rose tried to tell herself it was her imagination, but every time she entered the department he seemed to be on his way out. And when she was needed to work in Resus he always managed to send her on an errand—relatives needed reassuring, forms needed filling in, surgeons needed phoning. The excuses were endless. It was obvious that he didn't want to talk to her and she could only assume that he'd had second thoughts about what had happened on Saturday night. He, too, was afraid of the repercussions it might have if they furthered their relationship, and even though she shared his concerns it was painful to find herself being shut out all the time.

Friday rolled around and she went into work with a heavy heart. Fortunately, there was no time to dwell on the fact that it was her last day there because the department was heaving when she arrived. A school bus had collided with a delivery van and there were dozens of kids there who'd been injured.

'Can you take this lot to the treatment room and patch them up?' Charlie looked harassed as he led a convoy of teenage girls across the waiting area. Most had cuts on their faces because the windows of the bus had shattered and sprayed broken glass over them.

Rose grimaced. 'Some of those cuts look quite deep. Do we need the plastics reg down here?'

'See how you go, and give him a call if you feel you need a second opinion— OK, OK! I'm coming!'

Charlie hurried away to attend to another crisis. A group of teenage boys had started arguing, and Polly, the receptionist, was having a hard time keeping order. Rose briskly ushered her bunch towards the treatment room so they wouldn't be tempted to join in the fray.

'I'm going to see you all individually,' she explained, lining the girls up by the door. 'I want you to stay here until I call your name.'

'I don't want to be on my own,' one girl wailed. 'It's going to hurt, isn't it? You're going to stick needles into us and stitch up the cuts and—!'

'Fine! If you'd rather be seen together, you can all come in, but it will be a squash, I'm warning you.' She opened the door and waved them into the room. 'Put your school bags over there, then I'll have my first victim, please. Who's going to be the brave one?'

They all giggled at that, and she was relieved to see that the girl who'd been so upset even managed a smile. One of the group stepped forward so Rose made her sit on the couch while she cleaned the cut on her cheek with antiseptic. The wound wasn't very deep, and all it needed was a couple of butterfly strips to hold the edges together.

'That's you done. You can wait here for your friends, or go and get yourself a drink,' she suggested, washing her hands.

'There's a vending machine in the corridor that sells cans of soft drink.'

The girl decided to buy herself a drink, so that eased the situation a bit. Rose dealt with the next girl—another fairly minor cut—then she, too, left. The third girl had a much deeper cut on her neck, and Rose frowned as she finished cleaning it up.

'This is going to need a couple of stitches, I'm afraid. I'll need to numb the area first with a little local anaesthetic though.'

'Will it hurt?' the girl asked, looking scared out of her wits.

'All you'll feel is a little prick when I give you the injection,' Rose assured her. As a qualified nurse-practitioner she was allowed to give injections and do minor suturing, so she got everything ready and smiled reassuringly at the teenager. 'It will be all over in just a couple of minutes.'

She went to the couch but the girl—Tanya—shot to her feet. 'No, I don't want you to do it!'

'It's OK, there's nothing to be scared about.' Rose tried to reassure her, but the girl was terrified and pushed her away when she tried to calm her down.

'Everything all right in here?'

Rose glanced round when Rob poked his head round the door. 'Tanya isn't too happy about having an injection.'

'Not my most favourite fun thing to do either,' Rob observed cheerfully. 'Mind you, it will score you loads of points with your friends.'

'What do you mean?' Tanya demanded, looking a little starstruck at finding herself the centre of a young, good-looking doctor's attention.

'How many of your mates would have the bottle to sit there while they get stitches put in?' Rob treated the girl to a megawatt smile and Rose tried not to laugh. Rob certainly wasn't averse to ladling on the charm when it suited him!

'Not many,' Tanya replied scathingly.

'Then you need to show them what wimps they are, and I know the perfect way to do it, too. Have you got a mobile phone with a camera on it?' he asked. He carried on when Tanya nodded. 'Then we'll get your friend here to take some pictures. Your street cred will go right off the scale when your friends see them!'

Tanya looked thrilled by the idea. She didn't complain as Rose settled her on the couch again. One of her friends recorded every gory moment, from when the needle first went in to when the final suture was tied off. Everyone wanted their treatment recorded for posterity after that, so that Rose whizzed through the rest of the group in record time. Rob chuckled when she thanked him for his help after the girls had left.

'It's nice to know I can still make a maidenly heart flutter.'

'Oh, I think you proved that all right! If I were Suzanne, I'd keep a very close eye on you, Dr Lomax.'

'Suzie trusts me,' Rob said firmly. 'Knowing that the other person trusts you is one of the best things about being in a proper relationship, I've discovered. It makes a world of difference.'

He hurried away as there were still a lot of people who needed to be seen. Rose went back to the waiting room but she couldn't stop thinking about what Rob had said. It *did* make a difference when you knew that someone trusted you. Doubts wore away at a relationship and eventually destroyed it. Owen still had doubts about her. He might have apologised for the way he had treated her but he still wasn't convinced that she wouldn't hurt Daniel.

And it wasn't just Owen who had doubts either. She wasn't convinced that it would be a good thing to get more deeply involved with him when it could affect her relationship with Daniel. She had only just found Daniel again and she certainly wasn't willing to risk losing him. It left her with just one option, and that was to do nothing. She had to maintain the status quo and not start hoping for more than she had already achieved.

Saturday arrived and Owen was glad that he didn't have to go to work that day. It had been a stressful week and he desperately needed a respite from all the pressure. He didn't feel good about the way he had deliberately avoided Rose but he hadn't had a choice. He needed to keep his distance from her until he'd worked out what he intended to do.

Daniel had arranged to meet Rose again at the café near the Serpentine, so Owen waved him off and then made a start on restoring some sort of order to the garden. Laura had been a much keener gardener than him, and he'd let things lapse since she'd died. At least it would take his mind off Daniel's meeting with Rose. There really was no point wishing he could have gone to see her, too!

He had just gone back inside the house to make himself a sandwich a couple of hours later when he heard the front door slam. He poked his head round the kitchen door and was surprised to see Daniel standing in the hall. 'You're back early. I didn't think you'd be home for another couple of hours yet.'

'Rose didn't turn up.'

Daniel didn't say anything else as he ran up the stairs. Owen heard his bedroom door slam, then a second later music came thundering down through the ceiling. He had no idea what had happened, but it didn't need a genius to tell him that his son was upset—and no wonder, too, if Rose hadn't bothered to show up for their meeting.

His mouth compressed as he hurried up the stairs, because it was what he had feared would happen. He'd always been afraid that Rose would let Daniel down and now it seemed that she had. He knocked on the bedroom door and went in, trying to remember that it was Daniel's feelings that mattered, not his, but he couldn't help feeling bitterly disappointed in her.

'Are you sure you went to the right place?' he asked, reaching for the remote control and lowering the volume on the CD player so he could hear himself think. His head was already aching at the thought of Rose's perfidy without the music making matters any worse. Why had she agreed to see Daniel if she was going to let him down? Why had she made all those promises to *him* about putting Daniel's interests first if she hadn't meant them? And what other lies had she told if she'd told all those?

'Of course I'm sure! We arranged to meet at the Serpentine café at eleven o'clock.' Daniel glowered at him, but beneath the anger Owen could tell that he was deeply hurt. 'I know you think I'm totally useless, Dad, but even I couldn't make a mess of that!'

'I don't think you're useless at all.' Owen sat down on the end of the bed. 'Maybe Rose got it wrong. Maybe she went somewhere else. Where did you meet her last week?'

'The Tate Modern, and I tried there. And she wasn't at the British Museum either. In fact, I tried every single place we've ever met, but she wasn't at any of them!'

Daniel stared up at the ceiling, but Owen could see the glimmer of tears in his eyes and his anger ratcheted up another half-dozen notches. How could Rose have done this to him?

'Did you phone her? You had your mobile with you, didn't you?'

'Yes. I phoned her at home but she wasn't in. And she didn't phone me…although I'm not sure if I gave her my mobile phone number. Maybe she tried phoning here instead.' Daniel leapt to his feet, a dawning hope on his face as he raced across the room. 'You've been in the garden so you might not have heard the phone ringing. She might have left a message…'

He tore out of the room and Owen heard him thundering down the stairs. He followed more slowly, praying that Daniel was right and that Rose had left a message for him. Maybe she'd got held up or, worse still, wasn't feeling well. His heart thumped painfully at the thought as he hurried down to the hall, but all it took was one glance at Daniel's crestfallen expression to know that neither explanation was true.

'She hasn't phoned. There's no messages and I dialled 1471 to check who'd called and her number didn't come up.' Daniel dashed his hand across his eyes. 'She must have decided that she didn't want to see me any more.'

Owen tried to think of something encouraging to say but he honestly couldn't think of anything. And what point was there in making excuses for her? If Rose didn't want to see Daniel any more, it would be better if his son accepted it instead of building up false hopes for the future.

'I'm sorry, Daniel. I know you like Rose—'

'Forget it, Dad. You were never happy about me getting in touch with her, and now you've been proved right. I should have left her alone!'

Daniel brushed past him and ran back up the stairs to his room. Owen didn't follow him this time. The boy needed time on his own to adjust to what had happened.

Hell, *he* needed time to adjust to what had happened!

He swore under his breath, but harsh words couldn't ease the pain in his heart. Rose had let Daniel down and she'd let him down, too. She'd let him down so much that he hadn't even hit rock bottom yet, but he would do so at some point. At some point it would hit home to him what he had lost, and then it was going to hurt even more.

Rose was on her way to catch the bus when the phone rang. She snatched up the receiver, not wanting anything to delay her. She'd been so worn out after the stressful week that she'd over-slept. It had been a mad dash to get ready in time to go and meet Daniel, and she didn't want anything to hold her up.

'Rose Tremayne.'

Tucking the phone into the crook of her neck, Rose opened her purse and took out some money for her bus fare, then froze when the caller explained that she was phoning from the nursing-home where her father lived. Apparently he'd suffered a heart attack that morning and they thought she should know that the prognosis wasn't good.

Rose told the woman that she would get there as soon as she could and hung up, surprised by how upset she felt at the news. Her father had turned his back on her many years ago, but she still cared about him. She checked her watch and realised that if she hurried she might be able to catch the next train to Cornwall. She glanced at the phone but there was no time to phone Daniel and tell him what had happened. If she missed this train there wasn't another one until the evening. She would call him once she was on the train.

She made it to the station with just two minutes to spare. As soon as the train pulled out from the platform she took her mobile phone out of her bag, and groaned when she discovered that the battery was flat. She would have to wait until she got to the nursing-home now before she could phone Daniel, and he would wonder what had happened to her when she didn't show up. She could only hope he would understand, although she wasn't sure what Owen would think. Surely he would realise that she would never have willingly let Daniel down?

Daniel stayed in his room for the rest of the day, refusing any offers of food or other sustenance. Owen tried not to fuss, but it was worrying to see him on such a downward spiral after past experiences. When Daniel announced that he was going round to his friend's house that evening, it was all Owen could do not to ban him from going out. He knew it would be a mistake to let Daniel think he didn't trust him, but the memory of what had happened after Laura had died still haunted him. The last thing he wanted was Daniel ruining his life because of Rose!

Anger at the way Rose had behaved had been eating away at him all day long, so as soon as Daniel left he tried phoning her flat. There was no reply so he hung up and tried again later, but there was still no answer. Rose had seemingly disappeared off the face of the earth, and he couldn't help feeling concerned about her. The combination of worry and anger played havoc with his nerves, until in the end he decided that he would go round to her flat. For all he knew she could be lying there, desperately ill.

The thought was too much to bear. Owen got into his car and drove straight to her home. He tried ringing her doorbell, then tried several others when he got no response and finally struck lucky. One of Rose's neighbours had seen her getting into a taxi that morning and thought she'd heard Rose telling the driver to take her to the station.

Owen thanked the woman and got back into his car. So Rose wasn't ill—she'd gone off somewhere. She'd probably had a better offer—more exciting than a meeting with the son she'd had adopted. His anger soared, and it didn't help when he arrived home to find a message from her on the answering-machine, apologizing and explaining that she had been called away and that she would get in touch again at a later date.

Did she really think that she could just drop Daniel whenever it wasn't convenient for her to see him? he thought bitterly as he deleted the message. Obviously she must, but there was no way she was going to treat his son like that. She'd fulfilled all his prophecies—turned out exactly as he had feared she would—now all he could do was to make sure that she didn't try to worm her way back into Daniel's life. The only positive thing he could think of to come out of this was that he hadn't made the mistake of getting too involved with her. At least his heart wasn't broken...

Was it?

Rose felt completely drained by the time she got back to London the following evening. Her father had died in the early hours of Sunday morning without regaining consciousness, but at least she'd been with him at the end and that was some consolation. Now there were a lot of things she needed to do, but her first priority was to speak to Daniel.

There had been no one at home when she'd phoned the house the previous night, so she'd left a brief message, explaining that she would get in touch with him again later. Finding out that his grandfather was dying might have upset him, so she'd decided to break the news to him herself rather than tell him in a message.

She dialled the number, feeling herself well up with emotion when Owen answered. Just hearing his voice made her realise how much she longed to have him there with her. She'd been estranged from her father for a long time, but losing him had still hurt, and she desperately needed someone to comfort her.

'Yes? Who is this?'

Rose was jolted back to the present by the abrupt question. 'It's me—Rose. Is Daniel there? I'd like to speak to him, please.'

'I don't think so.'

His tone was harsh and she sighed. Obviously Owen was unhappy about her not showing up on Saturday, so maybe she should explain what had happened to him first. Once he knew the facts he would understand why she had decided not to tell Daniel what had happened in her message. 'Look, I'm sorry about Saturday but—'

'I'm not interested in your excuses. If you didn't want to see Daniel you should have told him that.'

'But I did want to see him! That's why I phoned and left that message—'

'To say that something had cropped up? I think he managed to work that out for himself.'

Once again he cut her off before she could finish explaining and she felt a cold chill envelop her. Owen wasn't interested in what she had to say because he'd already decided that she was at fault. She bit her lip when he continued in the same unforgiving tone. She wasn't going to try and justify her actions when he wasn't prepared to listen!

'Have you *any* idea how upset Daniel was when you didn't turn up?'

'Of course I have. That's why I want to speak to him now.'

'Well, I'm afraid that Daniel isn't interested in speaking to you any more than I am. You had your chance, Rose, and you blew it. Daniel doesn't want to hear from you again. And neither do I.'

He hung up before she could reply. Rose stared at the receiver in shock. It couldn't be true! Daniel would never have cut her out of his life like that...unless Owen had turned him against her?

Her heart started to ache at the thought. She didn't want to believe that Owen could be so cruel, but she couldn't ignore the fact that he had never been happy about her seeing Daniel. He'd always had reservations, and he seemed to have had even more after what had gone on after the party. He'd definitely been behaving very oddly since then, so maybe he'd seen this as the ideal solution. If she was removed from Daniel's life then she would be removed from his, too!

The thought that Owen might have resorted to such methods to get rid of her was incredibly painful, but her main concern was Daniel. She couldn't bear to imagine how hurt he must be feeling so she would write to him and explain what had happened. It might not be easy to convince him that she hadn't meant to let him down if Owen had put doubts into his mind, but she had to try, although she would be careful what she said.

She didn't want to create a rift between him and Owen, and certainly didn't want to put Daniel in the position of having to choose sides. Despite what Owen thought of her, she would never do anything to harm his relationship with his son. She cared too much about both of them to do that. And, because she cared, she would let Daniel decide what he wanted to do. Maybe he would want to see her again and maybe he wouldn't. But it would be his decision, not hers, and certainly not Owen's!

CHAPTER THIRTEEN

'I'VE received notification of a city-wide major incident training session. The powers that be have decided to make it as realistic as possible so that's why they have kept quiet about it. All I know is that it will be held some time this week.'

Owen glanced around the room, wondering if he looked as bad as he felt. It was almost two weeks since he'd last seen Rose and every second of every day was imprinted on his mind. It was as though her absence had taken all the colour out of his life and he couldn't bear to imagine how dark the future was going to be.

'So they're just going to land it on us, you mean?' Suzanne queried.

'That's right.' He forced himself to focus on the briefing, knowing how pointless it was to keep going over what had happened. He'd examined that last conversation they'd had in minute detail, *and* tortured himself with the thought that he should have listened to what she'd wanted to tell him. Maybe she'd had a valid reason for not turning up—extenuating circumstances he knew nothing about—and he'd not allowed her to explain. The thought made him feel more depressed than ever as he continued.

'We've had practice sessions in the past but they've always been planned months in advance. However, the one thing nobody can plan for is a major disaster. This will be the nearest we can get to the real thing.'

He turned to Rob, who was standing next to Suzanne. They had been inseparable since the night of the party and spent all their time in and out of work together. Now Owen had to batten down the pang of envy that assailed him. There was no likelihood of him and Rose being in that same situation so there was no point even thinking about it.

'I want you to act as our assessor and evaluate our response, Rob. We need to know that we are working to our maximum potential.'

'So I get to stand around holding a clipboard?' Rob pulled a face. 'Doesn't sound as though it's going to be a whole lot of fun.'

'We aren't doing it to have fun,' Owen reminded him shortly. 'This is an important exercise specifically to hone our skills. If you don't feel up to it, you'd better say so now.'

'No, it's fine,' Rob said hurriedly, looking suitably abashed.

'Good.' Owen didn't say anything else. There was no justification for taking out his ill-temper on the younger man. He thanked everyone and went to his office to phone the control centre. The St Anne's team was ready for action and now it was just a case of waiting for something to happen.

He sighed, because it felt as though he spent his whole life waiting for something to happen nowadays. Even his fears about Daniel going off the rails hadn't amounted to anything, although that was something he was happy about. The disappointment his son had suffered over Rose seemed to have had a galvanising effect, because Daniel had knuckled down to work and was making an effort to catch up so he could get the grades he needed for a place at university. In fact, Owen's main concern at the moment was that Daniel might be working too hard. He needed to take a break from studying, and Owen realised that he knew the perfect way he could do it, too.

Volunteers were needed to play the role of casualties during the forthcoming exercise, so he would ask Daniel if he was interested and put his name down. It would be nice to have him along, give them a chance to spend some time together as a family—only they weren't really a family, were they? Two people didn't make a family, although three would…

Owen's mouth compressed. He wasn't going down *that* route! Rose had gone out of their lives, and she'd gone for good.

Rose was undecided what she should do when she received notification of the training exercise. She'd been working at a hospital in the north of the city and she wasn't sure how they would feel if she was summoned away.

The past couple of weeks had been extremely hectic. She had made the arrangements for her father's funeral and travelled down to Cornwall for the service. There had been very few mourners at the church because most of her father's friends had died or moved away. However, the service had been a dignified ending to his life.

She'd decided to leave it to his solicitor to sort out his affairs. There would be some money coming from his estate once everything was settled but she didn't want it. It would be sent to a charity that helped homeless teenage mothers. She'd been in that situation herself and knew how it felt. If it meant that some other young girl wouldn't have to part with her baby, it would be money well spent.

She had written to Daniel, although she hadn't received a reply yet. She kept hoping that he would contact her but she knew how hurt he must have been. It was hard to deal with the thought that she might never see him again, and several times she'd picked up the phone to call him, but each time she had stopped herself. She didn't want to put him under any pressure when he was so vulnerable.

She hadn't spoken to Owen again. If he wanted her out of his life she had to respect his wishes, even though she knew in her heart that they could have had something very special if he'd only trusted her. But without trust love couldn't survive, so even if they had declared their feelings it wouldn't have made any difference in the end.

After a lot of thought, she decided to take part in the exercise. It would stop her brooding about what had happened, if nothing else. She'd been told the call could come at any hour of the day or night, but even so she was caught off guard when the phone went at midnight on Saturday, telling her to report to her designated command centre.

Rose got ready and made her way to the local hospital, where she was briefed along with everyone else who was taking part in the exercise. The scenario was a terrorist attack in the Docklands area of the city. Several bombs had exploded and a light aircraft had been flown into one of the tower blocks. Casualty figures were high and were expected to rise during the night.

Rose was assigned to a team and issued with protective clothing, then sent out to the ambulances. As she climbed on board she was reminded of the day she and Owen had travelled to the incident in the tube extension. Would he be there tonight? she wondered, and her heart leapt at the thought before she forced it to behave. Even if he was there there would be no touching reconciliation. That period of her life was over.

Owen had just switched off the bedside lamp when his pager beeped and he groaned as he got out of bed. He had been hoping to get an early night to make up for all the sleep he'd lost recently, thinking about Rose, but obviously he was out of luck.

He checked the display and frowned when he saw it was the prearranged signal for the major incident alert. He hadn't thought they would hold it at night, but if the authorities were aiming for realism it was probably the best time to do it. He woke Daniel, then got dressed and went downstairs.

Daniel came thundering down after him, obviously excited by the prospect of taking part. Owen had arranged to drop him off at the meeting point for would-be casualties so he drove there first.

'I'll see you back at home when we're finished,' he said as his son got out of the car. 'Just do what they tell you and be careful. No messing about and getting into trouble.'

'Chill out, Dad. This is going to be really cool so stop stressing.'

Daniel slammed the door and went bounding into the building. Owen shook his head as he put the car into gear. Chill out indeed!

Most of the St Anne's team had arrived by the time he got there, and once everyone had their protective clothing on they were driven to the scene of the purported incident. A large section of the Docklands area had been cordoned off and there were police and emergency services vehicles surrounding the training ground.

Owen led his team to the control centre where he was given a printed sheet of instructions. They were to deal with the injured who had been rescued from one of the tower blocks. Casualties were to be moved away from the building in case other explosive devices had been primed to go off at a later time. It was to be as realistic as possible and they were warned that there would be more explosions during the night.

'Right, you all know what to do. Work in pairs and listen out for any further instructions in case we have to evacuate the area. St Leonard's is receiving the walking wounded and St Anne's will take the more seriously injured. Anything specific—spinal injuries, those needing neurosurgery, etc.—refer to me. Is that clear?'

Nobody had any questions, so they made their way over to the scene. It was very realistic, with lots of casualties lying about. Owen knelt beside a young woman who had an open wound in her thigh, all beautifully staged with fake blood.

'Check her BP,' he told Sharon, who was working with him. 'We need to stop this bleeding and stabilise her.'

He attended to the woman and sent her off with the paramedics to the holding centre from where she would be transferred to hospital. Rob was standing nearby, taking notes, but Owen ignored him. They would have an in-depth discussion about how they'd fared after the exercise was over. He had just asked Sharon to splint a broken wrist when a policeman came hurrying over to him.

'Can you take a look at someone for me, Doc? I don't like the look of her at all.'

'You mean she's really ill?' Owen clarified as he followed the officer away from the scene. 'She's not one of our casualties?'

'Not from what I can tell.'

The policeman led him away from the training ground, ducking under a length of yellow tape which marked the boundary line. Owen hurried forward when he saw a figure lying on the ground near to some bushes. It was a young girl—not much older than Daniel, in fact—and she was bleeding heavily, although it wasn't until he rolled her over that he realised why.

'She's in labour and haemorrhaging badly from the look of her.' He checked her pulse and frowned when he felt how rapid and faint it was. 'Heaven knows how long she's been here, but she needs help.'

He broke off when the girl moaned. His heart sank when he lifted the hem of her blood-sodden dress. 'The baby's head has crowned. I'm going to need help to deliver it. Can you fetch one of the nurses over here, pronto?'

The policeman hurried away as Owen rapidly assessed the situation. Fortunately it was a mild night, so there was less risk of hypothermia, but the baby would need to be kept warm once it was born. His main concern was the amount of blood the mother had lost. She would need to be put on a drip...

'What do you want me to do?'

Owen's whole body jerked when he recognised Rose's voice. He could hardly believe his eyes when he looked up and saw her standing beside him. All he could think of was how much he had missed her and how wonderful it was to see her again. In that moment he realised something he'd tried desperately to deny: he loved her. So what did he do now?

Rose could feel the force of the emotions that were swirling around them and was afraid of what it might mean. Owen was staring at her as though he was in shock, and she knew that she had to do something to relieve the tension. She knelt down beside him, adopting her most professional tone in the hope that it would help.

'Shall I see to the baby while you attend to her?'

'Check that the cord isn't wrapped around the baby's neck.' The question seemed to have galvanised him into action and he quickly stood up. 'She's lost a lot of blood,' he said crisply. 'We'll need to set up a drip, so I'll fetch what we need.'

'Fine.' Rose took a steadying breath as he hurried away. She'd managed to overcome the first hurdle and now she had to get on and do her job. She carefully inserted her finger into the birth canal and checked that the umbilical cord wasn't looped around the baby's neck and in danger of strangling it. Owen came back with the fluid but she didn't look at him because she didn't want anything to distract her.

'There's no sign of the cord,' she told him when he crouched down beside her.

'Good. That's one less thing to worry about. Put this under her, will you? It will help to protect the baby when he's born.'

He handed her a blanket, then bent over and swabbed the back of the girl's hand. She was semi-conscious and didn't seem to know what was happening as he inserted a cannula. He attached it to a bag of saline and looped the handle over the branch of a nearby bush.

Rose quickly spread the blanket on the ground, sliding it

under the girl's hips. She was having a contraction, and Rose placed her hand on her belly, feeling her muscles straining.

'How's the baby doing?'

Rose felt her heart lurch when Owen leant over her so that he could see what was happening. She could feel the warmth of his breath on the back of her neck and shivered. 'It's difficult to tell without a foetal monitor,' she said flatly, because she couldn't risk any hint of emotion creeping into her voice.

'Not something we brought along on this little jaunt, unfortunately,' he observed dryly. He knelt down beside her, using his stethoscope to listen to the baby's heartbeat, and shook his head. 'I'm not happy with either of them. The child's heartbeat is way too fast, which means it's in distress, and the mum's lost an awful lot of blood. We need to deliver this child sooner rather than later.'

Rose frowned as she watched him open his case. 'What are you going to do?'

'Get things along a bit. The perineum hasn't stretched enough and that's what is holding up the proceedings. If I make a *small* cut—an episiotomy—in the perineum, that should help speed up the birth.'

He drew up an injection of anaesthetic and quickly administered it, then used sterile scissors to make a cut in the perineum—the tissue between the vagina and the anus. Rose sighed in relief when the baby's head immediately moved further down the birth canal.

'That seems to have done the trick!'

'It does.' Owen placed his hand under the infant's head to support it, his touch so gentle and so tender that Rose felt a lump come to her throat. He cared so much about the people he treated that it was a truly moving experience to work with him.

The girl's contractions were coming faster now, her body heaving as she struggled to deliver her child. Rose squeezed her hand, willing her to find the strength to make that final effort.

The baby suddenly slithered out into Owen's hands and immediately began to cry. It was a little boy, and he seemed remarkably healthy despite his inauspicious start in life.

'My baby?' the girl whispered, rousing herself when she heard her child's cries.

'It's a little boy,' Rose told her. 'And he sounds absolutely fine to me.'

'Thank you…' Tears suddenly poured down the girl's cheeks and she couldn't say anything else, but Rose understood. She remembered only too clearly how she'd felt when Daniel had been born.

She looked up, and she could tell immediately that Owen knew what she was thinking. There was a connection between them still and it hadn't gone away. In that moment she knew that she had to tell him why she hadn't kept her appointment with Daniel that day. Maybe it wouldn't change his opinion of her, but she couldn't bear it if he never knew the truth.

She cleaned the baby and wrapped him in a blanket once the cord had been cut. The policeman was despatched to fetch an ambulance and mother and baby were loaded on board. Rose took a final look at the infant, her emotions see-sawing when she recalled the moment when she'd held Daniel in her arms for the very first time. Her love for him had been instantaneous and it had never faded. He was her son and she loved him with all her heart. If she achieved nothing else that night, she would make Owen believe that.

'Take care of yourself,' she told the girl in a voice that was husky with emotion. 'And take care of that gorgeous little boy, too.'

'I shall.' The girl gave her a radiant smile as the paramedics closed the doors. 'I don't know what's going to happen to us but I'm going to look after him the very best way I can!'

Rose couldn't answer, she was too choked up. She'd made that same promise herself eighteen years ago, but she hadn't kept it. She should have tried harder, should have found a way to work through her problems and not had Daniel adopted…

'Don't!'

She looked round in surprise when she heard the anguish in Owen's voice. 'I'm sorry?'

'You're torturing yourself with the thought that you should have done things differently when Daniel was born, and I can't bear it, Rose. I can't bear to see you suffering like that!'

He swung round and strode back to where he'd left his case, but she couldn't let him leave without explaining that comment. Why should it matter to him if she suffered? Why did he care?

It felt as though her heart was going to burst right out of her chest as she ran after him, but it was imperative that he answer her questions. 'I don't understand, Owen. Why do you care how I feel? You made it perfectly clear what you thought of me the last time we spoke.'

'Yes, I did,' he ground out, and the anger in his voice almost made her back down. But from somewhere deep inside herself she found the courage to carry on.

'You still believe that I let Daniel down, don't you?'

'Do you blame me?'

He tried to step around her but she wouldn't let him pass. 'No, I don't blame you for that. I blame you for not listening to what I wanted to tell you. I blame you for not trusting me and for always doubting my sincerity.' Her voice caught but she made herself continue. 'And I blame myself even more for caring what you think when I shouldn't give a damn about your feelings!'

CHAPTER FOURTEEN

OWEN knew there were many points in that statement which he should have homed in on, but it was just one point he was interested in, the last one: Rose cared how he felt?

He tried to deal with the idea rationally but it was impossible. It wasn't the kind of thought he could take his time to consider. It was big and bold, and it needed his immediate attention.

'What do you mean, you care how I feel?' he shot back. 'If you'd taken any account of my feelings, we wouldn't be in this mess!'

'And whose fault is that? If you'd let me explain what had happened we could have sorted this out.'

'You mean if I'd been stupid enough to listen to a pack of lies,' he scoffed.

'I have never lied to you. And I have never lied to Daniel either,' she said quietly. 'I have told you the truth right from the beginning, but obviously you don't believe me. I just hope that you won't try to turn Daniel against me. I agreed to play fair, Owen, and I hope you will, too.'

She turned and walked away, but there was no way that he was prepared to let her claim the moral high ground. She was the one at fault—not him!

He raced after her, but he'd only gone a couple of steps when there was a loud explosion from one of the buildings.

Owen stopped dead when he saw a stream of 'casualties' staggering out of the doors. It looked as though the next round in the proceedings had begun. He glanced at Rose, who had stopped as well.

'I need to get back to my team, but at some point we're going to have to talk about this.'

'What for? You never believe a word I say, Owen, so why bother?'

'Because this situation is driving me mad—that's why!'

He hurried away before she could ask him to explain what he meant. He'd already said more than he'd intended to, and definitely more than was wise. Letting Rose know that she had the power to hurt him could be a mistake when she might use it to her advantage.

He frowned, because that idea simply didn't gel with what he knew about her. He had never seen her behave cruelly towards anyone. She was gentle and kind and really cared about people, so why should he imagine that she would try to hurt him?

Owen's head began to spin, because he was no longer sure about anything any more. He had immediately assumed the worst when Rose hadn't showed up for her meeting with Daniel, but what if there had been a genuine reason why she hadn't been able to get there—circumstances he knew nothing about? The thought that he might have done her a huge disservice was more than he could bear, and he knew that he had to find out what had really happened. He owed it to all of them to do that—Rose, Daniel and himself.

Rose made her way back to where her team was working, feeling her heart beating in heavy, jerky thuds. She knew it would be foolish to read too much into what Owen had said to her but she couldn't help it. Was he having second thoughts about her, perhaps?

The thought was just too much to deal with right then. She

knew that she had to put it out of her mind while she got on with her job. When her section leader asked her to help with the new group of casualties who were being treated, she immediately agreed. It was absolute mayhem when she got there, with bodies lying around all over the place. The make-up artists had done a brilliant job, too, and the injuries were horribly realistic.

Rose made her way to the edge of the group where a young man was lying on the ground, groaning. He'd been made up to appear as though he had massive abdominal injuries, right down to the fake intestines spilling out of his abdominal cavity. Abdominal injuries were always the worst kind of injury because so many vital organs could be damaged, so she ran a mental checklist as she knelt beside him.

She had to control the bleeding and minimise the risk of infection. The intestine would also need to be protected to avoid it being perforated…

Her mind seized up when the casualty rolled over and she suddenly realised it was Daniel. She couldn't seem to move as she stared at him in horror. There was a buzzing in her ears and the ground seemed to be rushing up towards her…

'It's OK. He isn't really hurt, Rose. Look at him.'

All of a sudden Owen was there and she turned to him with all the horror she felt clearly visible on her face. 'It's Daniel,' she whispered.

'I know, but he's not really hurt, Rose. This isn't real, sweetheart, it's make-believe. Trust me. I wouldn't lie to you about this, would I? It's too important.'

He knelt down beside her and gripped her hand tightly in his, and that was what finally got through to her. Rose took a shuddering breath as she looked at her son and saw the alarm on his face.

'I'm OK, Rose. Really, I am. It's just some fake gore and guts. Look.'

He picked up the loop of intestine and waggled it about to show her that it was just a bit of plastic tubing. Rose laughed at her own foolishness, only once she'd started laughing she couldn't seem to stop. Owen put his arm around her and gently helped her to her feet.

'You need to take some time out,' he said firmly as he led her over to the rest area and helped her duck under the tape. The WVS had set up a tea-stall and he sat her down by a wall, then fetched her a piping hot cup of tea. 'Drink this. I've put three spoons of sugar in it, so it will probably taste vile, but it will do you good.'

She took a sip of the tea and shuddered. 'You're right—it does taste awful.'

'It makes a change, then. It's not often I'm right nowadays. I seem to have got an awful lot of things wrong recently, haven't I?'

'I never meant to hurt Daniel,' she said urgently, the tears spilling over and trickling down her face because it was so important that he believe her this time.

'I know.' He bent and kissed her on her forehead, and his lips were so gentle that she closed her eyes as pain washed over her. She couldn't bear to have him kiss her this way if he didn't mean it. She loved him so much, and if he didn't love her then she didn't know what she was going to do.

He drew back and looked at her. 'So what really happened, Rose? Why didn't you meet Daniel as you'd arranged?'

She placed her hand on top of his, needing the contact more than anything at that moment. When she was touching him she could make herself believe that things would work out the way she wanted them to.

'My father had a heart attack and I had to travel down to Cornwall. It was such a rush to get to the station that I didn't have time to phone Daniel before I left. I intended to ring him once I was on the train, but the battery on my mobile was flat.

I tried phoning your house that evening, but there was nobody in so I left that message. I didn't want to say too much in case I upset him, so that's why I didn't say anything about my father.'

'I see.' He took a deep breath and let it out on a sigh. 'Daniel had gone round to his friend's house. He was really cut up when you didn't turn up.'

'I know, and I am so sorry, Owen. It's the last thing I wanted to happen. But there was nothing I could do once I'd got on the train. And when I got to the nursing-home the doctor was there so I couldn't ring him then—'

'No. You don't have to explain. I know how difficult it is when someone is seriously ill.' He squeezed her hand. 'I'm sorry, Rose. I should have listened when you tried to tell me what had happened. How is your father now? Is he any better?'

She bit her lip when she felt the tears welling up again. 'He…he died on the Sunday morning,' she told him in a broken little voice.

'Hell!' He pulled her to him and held her close. 'I am *so* sorry. It must have been a terrible ordeal for you, having to go through that on your own. And to think that I tore a strip off you, too—' He broke off and she felt him shudder.

'You did what you thought was right at the time, Owen.'

'But that doesn't excuse the way I behaved. I didn't even tell Daniel that you'd phoned or left a message. I just took it upon myself to decide what was best for him.' He shook his head. 'I don't know how he's going to feel when he finds out about your father. He'll be really upset.'

'He already knows,' she said quietly. 'I wrote to him and explained what had happened.'

'Did you?' He drew back and looked at her in surprise. 'Daniel didn't mention anything about a letter to me. How odd.'

'Maybe he didn't think it was worth telling you about it if he'd decided not to see me again.' She had to stop because there was a lump in her throat and she couldn't go on.

'I can't believe that. Are you sure he received it? We've had a lot of problems with our post recently.'

'I'm sure he did.' Rose shook her head. She refused to start clutching at straws. She had to accept that Daniel might never want to see her again, and if that was the case, it meant that she and Owen couldn't see each other either. Even if he had accepted that she was telling him the truth now, there was no way they could be together if Daniel didn't want anything more to do with her. It would put far too great a strain on his relationship with Owen.

'It's far more likely that Daniel has decided that he doesn't want to see me any more. I don't blame him because you've just told me how upset he was.'

'But that's crazy! I'll talk to him and explain what happened—tell him about your phone call and the message—'

'No. Please don't do that. I don't want you to tell him.'

'But why not?'

'Because it has to be his decision.' She shrugged, trying not to let him see how hard this was for her. But she couldn't bear to think that Daniel might blame his father if he found out that Owen had interfered. 'I've told him what happened and it's up to him what he intends to do.'

'You make it sound as though you don't really care if you see him again,' Owen said slowly, as though he couldn't quite believe what he was hearing.

'It isn't a question of what I want. It's what is best for all of us,' she said flatly. How could she possibly explain that she was trying to save him from getting hurt as well as Daniel? Owen had never made her any promises: he hadn't said that he wanted her to be a part of his life so she could have completely misread the situation. Just because he'd kissed her a few times, it didn't mean he wanted to spend his life with her!

It was hard to hide the pain that thought caused her, but Rose knew that she would never forgive herself if she ended up hurting the two people she loved most of all. 'It might be best if we all went back to the way we were,' she said quietly. 'That way you and Daniel can get on with your lives and I can get on with mine.'

'And ne'er the twain shall meet.' He laughed harshly as he let her go and stood up. 'You could be right, Rose, and who am I to argue? I certainly can't claim to be an expert at sorting out problems with my track record. Anyway, I'd better get back and see how everyone is doing.'

He walked away, not looking back as he ducked under the tape and went back to the training ground. Rose finished her tea, but the ache in her heart didn't ease. Maybe she had done the right thing for all of them, but it still hurt. And this kind of pain took a lifetime to heal.

It was the middle of the afternoon before Owen got home. The exercise had been a huge success, although there were a few issues that needed to be addressed. There would be a meeting for all those who had taken part at some point, but at the moment he just wanted to go home and lock himself away.

He let himself into the house, sighing when he heard the sound of music coming from upstairs. Obviously Daniel was home, and although he loved his son dearly he could have done with a couple of hours on his own to think about what Rose had said to him.

He still couldn't understand why she had turned her back on Daniel. He'd seen for himself last night just how much Daniel meant to her. If he'd had doubts about her sincerity before, he didn't have them now. She loved the boy just as much as he did, so why was she willing to let him go? And why had she refused his offer to intercede on her behalf? It didn't make sense.

Owen cursed roundly as he filled the kettle and made himself some coffee. Daniel must have heard him moving about the kitchen because he came thundering down the stairs.

'Want a cup?' Owen asked.

'No, it's OK, thanks. I had some when I got in.'

Daniel pushed his hands into the pockets of his jeans and slouched against the doorframe. Owen forbore to tell him to either come into the room or go out, as he usually did. This wasn't the time for one of his parental lectures. Maybe Rose was prepared to let Daniel take the initiative, but the very least he could do was to make sure his son had all the facts before him. He was just working himself up to confess what he'd done when Daniel spoke.

'I saw Rose again before I came home.'

'Did you?' Owen felt his insides churning. Daniel obviously wanted to tell him something and he couldn't help wondering what it was.

'Yes. I decided that I needed to talk to her, so I went to find her.' Daniel shrugged. 'She told me what had happened the other week and why she couldn't meet me as we'd arranged.'

'Her father had a heart attack,' Owen said softly, seeing the flicker of pain that crossed Daniel's face.

'It must have been really awful for her. I know that she and her father weren't on speaking terms for years—'

'But he was still her father and she cared about him,' Owen finished for him.

'Exactly. Anyway, I'm glad that I spoke to her because it's helped me sort everything out in my head. I've been a bit down recently because I thought she didn't care about me.'

'Rose loves you very much. You saw that for yourself last night. She was absolutely panic stricken when she realised that you were one of the casualties.'

'I know. That's what made me decide to talk to her.'

'I'm glad you did,' Owen said truthfully. 'It would be a real shame if you two stopped seeing each other because of some unfortunate misunderstanding...' He suddenly stopped and frowned. 'Hang on a minute. Rose told me that she'd written to you and explained what had happened. Didn't you get her letter?'

'Yes, I got it.'

'And?' he prompted.

'And I tore it up.' Daniel came and sat down at the table. Owen sighed when he saw how guilty he looked.

'Without reading it first, I assume?' He shook his head when Daniel nodded. 'You should have read it, son. Then you would have known what had happened.'

'I know, but I was really peeved at the time because Rose hadn't even tried to phone me.'

'Yes, she did. She left a message on Saturday night to say that she'd been called away.' He paused, but there was no way that he could avoid telling Daniel the truth to save face. 'She also phoned again on Sunday, when she got back to London, to speak to you.'

'She did? But why didn't you tell me?'

'Because at the time I was so angry with her for letting you down that I refused to listen to what she was trying to tell me. I had no idea what had gone on until last night, in fact.'

'I can't believe you never told me that she'd phoned!' Daniel shot to his feet. 'I'm not a kid, Dad. I'm old enough to make my own decisions. It was up to me to decide if I wanted to speak to Rose, not you!'

'I know. And I'm sorry. I'm not going to try and justify my actions by claiming I was doing it for your own good because I shouldn't have interfered.'

'So why did you?' Daniel sat down again. 'You've been acting very strangely ever since you met Rose, and it's not like you. You've had a real downer on her even though she's done nothing wrong. OK, so she had me adopted, but she did it for the very best of reasons and you can't blame her for that. Why do you dislike her so much?'

'I don't.' Owen's head began to throb. He didn't dislike

Rose—just the opposite, in fact. But he couldn't tell Daniel that. 'I was afraid that you'd get hurt. It was a terrible shock for you when Mum died, and I was worried in case it tipped you over the edge again.'

Daniel grimaced. 'I'm not stupid. I know I went off the rails but I'm not going to do it again. So was that it? You were worried about the effect it could have had on me?'

'No.' He took a deep breath because this was the hardest part of all to admit. 'I was also afraid that I could end up losing you. My whole world fell apart when your mother died and I was desperate to hang on to what I had left. Rose was a threat…or so it seemed to me at first.'

'But once you got to know her you realised she wasn't a threat?'

'Yes.' Owen sighed. 'Rose thinks the world of you, Daniel, and she wouldn't do anything to hurt you.'

'I think I've always known that, deep down inside. I'm just so glad that we managed to clear things up last night. Although I don't know why she didn't tell me herself about those phone calls, do you?'

'I've no idea, to be honest.' He frowned. 'She even asked me not to tell you, and it doesn't make sense, does it?'

'So Rose asked you specifically not to tell me that she'd phoned?'

'Yes. She was adamant that she didn't want me to say anything and I wish I knew why.'

'Then maybe you and Rose need to talk to each other.' Daniel stood up and grinned at him. 'I had a feeling there was something going on from a few things Rose said, and this just confirms it.'

'Confirms what?' Owen demanded, but Daniel just laughed.

'Work it out, Dad. You'll get there in the end!' He bounded out of the room, taking the stairs two at a time so that it sounded as though a herd of elephants was stampeding through the house.

Owen frowned as he tried to follow his son's advice. Rose

had made it clear from the outset that she would fight tooth and nail to see her son, so why had she been prepared to walk away if Daniel hadn't wanted to see her again? And why had she insisted that he mustn't tell Daniel about his part in recent events? That didn't make any sense at all…unless she'd been afraid that if he'd told Daniel it could have had an impact on *his* relationship with him?

Owen gasped. It was as if a light had been switched on and he could see the situation clearly at last. Rose hadn't wanted to risk harming his relationship with Daniel and *that* was why she had asked him not to say anything. He could understand why she would want to protect Daniel, but was it possible that she had wanted to protect him, too? She'd admitted that she cared about his feelings, but maybe there was more to it than that: maybe she cared about *him?*

All of a sudden he knew that he had to find out the truth. He would go to see Rose and ask her point blank how she felt. And if her answer was what he hoped it would be, then…

He cut off the rest of that thought. He wasn't going to make the mistake of tempting fate!

Rose had just made herself a cup of coffee when the doorbell rang. She pressed the button on the intercom speaker and was stunned when she heard Owen's voice asking her to let him in. She had no idea what he wanted…unless he'd found out that Daniel had spoken to her again?

Her heart sank. It had been so wonderful to be able to sort out all the misunderstandings that had led to their recent estrangement, and she couldn't bear to think that something might go wrong at this stage. Surely Owen now understood that she only wanted what was best for the boy? Even if she and Owen hadn't parted on the friendliest of terms last night, she couldn't believe that he still had doubts about her integrity. But why else had he come?

The thought made her feel so emotionally raw that she knew

she couldn't bear to see him. Maybe she would be able to deal with this later but not now.

'I'm sorry, Owen, but this really isn't a good time. I'm too tired to speak to you—'

'I know you're tired, Rose, but it's absolutely vital that I talk to you,' he said urgently—so urgently, in fact, that she was immediately alarmed.

'Has something happened to Daniel?' she demanded.

'Daniel is fine. He's at home, deafening the neighbours with his music.' He paused, and her pulse leapt when she heard how his voice grated when he continued. 'This concerns you and me, not Daniel.'

Rose had no idea what he meant, yet she couldn't find it in her heart to turn him away when he sounded so desperate. She unlocked the main doors, then waited in the hall until he knocked on her door.

'I need to ask you something, Rose,' he said as soon as he had stepped inside the flat. 'But first of all I want you to promise me that you will give me a truthful answer.'

'If I can,' she murmured, not sure what she was agreeing to.

'Why did you ask me not to tell Daniel about that message and the phone call?'

'I already explained it to you,' she said shortly, turning to go back to the kitchen because the expression in his eyes was playing havoc with her composure. Why was he looking at her as though she held his whole future in her hands? It didn't make sense.

'I know you did, but I don't think you told me the full story, did you?'

His tone was achingly gentle and she bit her lip. It was hard not to blurt it all out then: how she'd wanted to protect his relationship with Daniel; how she'd wanted to protect *him*. 'I can't see any point in this, Owen. We've said everything that needs to be said.'

'No, we haven't. We haven't even touched on the really important issue, which is that I love you.' He turned her to face him and her heart started to race when she saw the warmth in his eyes. 'I love you, Rose Tremayne. I don't know how it happened but it's true.'

'You love me?' she said.

'Yes. Is it really such a shock to hear me say that?' He stared into her eyes and Rose felt a flood of emotions run through her. She wanted to believe that he was telling her the truth but she was afraid of getting hurt.

'Of course it's a shock,' she said, stepping back so that he was forced to release her. 'You've never made any secret of how you felt about me, Owen, have you?'

'No. And it's something I shall regret until my dying day, too.' He ran a hand through his hair and she was shocked to see how it trembled. 'I've behaved very badly towards you, Rose, and I understand why you find it hard to believe what I'm saying, but it's true. I love you with the whole of my heart.'

'I want to believe you,' she whispered, feeling the hot sting of tears burning her eyes.

'But you're worried in case it's some kind of a trick?' he suggested, and the agony in his voice made her reach out to him.

'No!' she said, clinging tightly to his hand. 'I know you would never do anything as cruel as that.'

'Thank you.' He lifted her hand to his mouth and kissed her fingers with infinite tenderness. 'The fact that you can still trust me after everything that's happened means more to me than I can say.'

'You were only ever trying to protect Daniel,' she said huskily.

'I was, but I went about it the completely wrong way. I saw you as a threat and you were never that, were you?'

'No. And I never wanted to come between you and Daniel either,' she said fiercely, desperate to convince him.

'I know that now. That's why you didn't want me to tell Daniel about those phone calls, wasn't it? You were worried in case it damaged my relationship with him when he found out what I'd done.'

'I couldn't bear to think that you two might fall out because of me. Daniel needs you, Owen.'

'And I need him, too. I told him that after I'd explained what I'd done.'

'And how did he take it?' she said anxiously.

'He was angry at first, of course. But I think he's forgiven me now for interfering.' He kissed her hand again. 'He told me that he'd spoken to you and that you'd sorted things out. I'm so glad, Rose.'

'So am I. I was afraid that he would never want to see me again,' she admitted.

'Yet you still wouldn't let me tell him about the part I played?' He drew her to him and looked deep into her eyes. 'Were you just worried about damaging my relationship with him or was there another reason for that, sweetheart?'

'I…I didn't want to cause a rift between you two,' she said, avoiding his eyes because she wasn't sure what he might see in hers. She couldn't begin to explain how wonderful it had felt to hear him using that tender endearment.

'You won't ever do that. I think Daniel has a far better understanding of the situation than either of us have given him credit for.' He drew her into his arms and dropped a kiss on her nose. 'Do you care about me, Rose, just a little bit?'

'Of course I care. You're Daniel's father.'

'And that's all I am to you?'

'Isn't it enough?'

'No, it isn't. I want you to care about me, Rose, the person I am here.' He pressed her hand against his heart and held it there so she could feel it beating against her palm. 'I want you to love me as much as I love you but I'm not sure if it's possible after what I've done. I hurt you, Rose, and I will spend the rest of my life trying to make amends if you'll let me.'

'I don't want you to make amends for anything,' she whispered, unbearably moved by his words.

'Because you don't feel the same way I do?'

'No, because it isn't necessary for you to make amends. You don't need to apologise for caring about our son, Owen.'

'Don't I?' He brushed her mouth with a kiss then smiled at her. 'So does that mean that you might be able to love me just a little bit?'

'I might.'

'Well, it's a start at least.' Another kiss, only this time it lasted rather longer so that Rose was trembling when he drew back. 'So how little are we talking about? I mean, I love you totally and completely, so that's a pretty expansive feeling. Is there any reason to hope that you might be able to meet me halfway?'

'Only halfway?' Rose chuckled as happiness suddenly bubbled up inside her. 'That doesn't sound like the Owen Gallagher I know. You aren't a man who normally settles for half-measures.'

'Not normally, no. But this is very different to the usual run-of-the-mill scenarios. I don't go round asking women if they love me every day of the week, so you need to be patient with me.'

'How patient do you want me to be?' she responded, reaching up so she could kiss him. She smiled when she felt him shudder. 'And how many more questions are you planning to ask me?'

'None. I've asked the only important one. So, Rose, you think you could love me?'

'Yes, I think so.'

'And how long would I need to wait before you're sure?'

'That depends.'

'On what?' One dark bow arched arrogantly.

'On what kind of incentives you're offering to help me make

up my mind.' She smiled. 'Talking has never been one of our strong points, has it, Owen? We usually end up arguing, so it might be safer not to go down that route.'

'Hmm, I see. Obviously I need to work out a plan of action—come up with some better tactics.'

He suddenly bent and swept her into his arms, ignoring her startled gasp as he carried her into the sitting room and set her on the sofa. He sat down beside her and took her in his arms. 'Try this for starters. If it doesn't work, we can try something else.'

'Something else—' she began, but it was difficult to have a rational discussion when his mouth had claimed hers in a kiss that immediately stole her ability to string two words together. Rose sighed blissfully when he raised his head. 'That was rather nice.'

'Nice?' He drew back in affront. 'It was more than nice. It was brilliant!'

'Sorry!' She laughed, loving this new, gentler side he was showing her. The old Owen Gallagher would never have teased her this way and it was wonderful to know that he could be so open with her. 'I didn't mean to put a dent in your ego. Anyway, nice is a lovely word.'

'It seems a bit half-hearted to me,' he grumbled, pulling her back into his arms. 'I'm aiming for a full-blown assault on your emotions, not some half-hearted little tin-pot campaign.'

He kissed her again, and there was nothing half-hearted about this kiss. This kiss would have turned any woman's head—and she wasn't just any woman. She was the woman Owen had just confessed to love, and that made her feel very special indeed.

Reaching up, she wrapped her arms around his neck and kissed him back. She had no doubts about how she felt and she showed him that through her kiss. She loved him, too, loved and wanted him, and just being in his arms was the most wonderful thing that had ever happened to her... apart from finding Daniel, of course.

Tears suddenly streamed down her face and Owen pulled back in alarm. 'Rose! Darling, what have I done?'

'Nothing. It's not your fault,' she murmured, laughing and crying at the same time. 'Well, yes, it is. It's you and Daniel, and how happy I feel…'

She couldn't go on, but he understood. His own voice was thickened with emotion. 'I feel the same way. I have Daniel and I've found you. I never thought I could be this happy again.'

'I'm so glad. I know how much you loved Laura, and I swear that I won't ever feel jealous of what you had with her.' She kissed him tenderly, meaning every word. 'Even if you can only feel for me a fraction of the love you felt for Laura, I'll be happy.'

He returned her kiss and his eyes were brimming with tears when he looked at her. 'I loved Laura, and I always will love her. But loving her doesn't mean that I can't love you, Rose. I love you just as much, and I want to spend the rest of my life showing you how I feel.'

'Then I think I can meet you more than halfway.' She smiled up at him with her heart in her eyes. 'I love you, Owen. I just want to be with you and make you happy, if you'll let me. I was so afraid of telling you how I felt because I knew we couldn't be together if Daniel didn't want to see me any more.' Her voice broke. 'I would never have done anything to hurt you or him.'

'I… You… Oh, hell!'

He swept her into his arms and kissed her, leaving her no room for any doubts as his lips plundered hers. Yet even though his mouth demanded a response it also told her how much he cared about her, too. When he stood up and held out his hand Rose didn't hesitate. She let him lead her into her bedroom and knew it was what she wanted more than anything. She wanted to put the seal on their love because this would be the commitment they both needed.

Owen slowly undressed her, taking his time as he helped her

out of her blouse and jeans. His eyes grazed over her, hot with desire and tender with love, and she shivered.

'You're so beautiful, Rose,' he whispered, tracing the curve of her breast with a gentle finger. His hand moved lower, passing lightly over her belly. 'Even more beautiful because you're the reason I have Daniel. Thank you for being brave enough to give him up. My life wouldn't have been the same without him.'

Rose was so touched that she couldn't speak, but she didn't need words to tell him how she felt. When he stripped off his clothes and took her in his arms, she showed him how much he meant to her. They made love with a tenderness that made them both cry, but they were healing tears. They had both suffered terrible losses in their lives but they had found each other now.

Rose kissed him on the mouth then looked deep into his eyes. 'I love you and I want to be with you from now on. I know we will have to take things slowly because of Daniel, but I don't want there to be any mistake about how I feel.'

'There won't be, because I love you, too.'

Owen kissed her back, and the kiss was about to lead to something more when the phone suddenly rang. They both froze when they heard the answering-machine cut in, followed by a familiar voice leaving a message.

'Hi, Rose. Hi, Dad. I just wanted to check that you guys were OK. Don't worry about me, I'm fine. I'm going to do some studying. Somebody is going to have to keep you two in your dotage! Anyway, have fun and be careful—although a baby brother or sister could help to keep you on your toes while I'm at uni!'

The message ended and Rose looked at Owen in horror. 'I'm not on the Pill!'

'Oh!' He burst out laughing. 'I don't know how we're going to live it down if you get pregnant. When I think of all the lectures I've given Daniel about having safe sex…!'

Rose giggled. 'We're going to look like a real pair of idiots, aren't we?'

'We are. Although it would be worth it.' He kissed the tip of her nose. 'I can't think of anything I'd like more than to have another child with you, Rose.'

'Me, too,' she agreed dreamily, her mind full of delicious thoughts of babies.

'There's just one proviso, though.'

'And that is?'

'We have to get married.' His expression was stern all of a sudden. 'We want to set a good example for Daniel, don't we?'

'I don't think Daniel needs us to show him the way. You've brought him up so well that he knows what's right.'

'So you're saying that you don't want to marry me?'

'No. I'm saying that I will marry you because I want to, not for any other reason.' She kissed him softly. 'My answer is yes, Owen, so do you think we should celebrate?'

'Oh, yes! Celebrations are definitely in order!'

The Times, Saturday 19th March
Gallagher. To Rose (née Tremayne) and Owen, a daughter, Carys. A precious sister for Daniel. Mother and daughter both well, father and brother ecstatic!

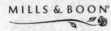

0606/108/MB038

Escape to...

19th May 2006

16th June 2006

21st July 2006

18th August 2006

*Available at WH Smith, Tesco, ASDA, Borders, Eason, Sainsbury's
and all good paperback bookshops*

www.millsandboon.co.uk

FREE

4 BOOKS AND A SURPRISE GIFT!

We would like to take this opportunity to thank you for reading this Mills & Boon® book by offering you the chance to take FOUR more specially selected titles from the Medical Romance™ series absolutely FREE! We're also making this offer to introduce you to the benefits of the Reader Service™—

- ★ **FREE home delivery**
- ★ **FREE gifts and competitions**
- ★ **FREE monthly Newsletter**
- ★ **Books available before they're in the shops**
- ★ **Exclusive Reader Service offers**

Accepting these FREE books and gift places you under no obligation to buy; you may cancel at any time, even after receiving your free shipment. Simply complete your details below and return the entire page to the address below. You don't even need a stamp!

YES! Please send me 4 free Medical Romance books and a surprise gift. I understand that unless you hear from me, I will receive 6 superb new titles every month for just £2.80 each, postage and packing free. I am under no obligation to purchase any books and may cancel my subscription at any time. The free books and gift will be mine to keep in any case.

M6ZEE

Ms/Mrs/Miss/Mr...Initials ....
BLOCK CAPITALS PLEASE

Surname ....

Address ....

....

....Postcode ....

Send this whole page to:
The Reader Service, FREEPOST CN81, Croydon, CR9 3WZ